THE WAGG

Summer Edition

Ah, 'tis the season. The crème de la crème has arrived for three months of decadence. After all, who would miss the beginning of polo season? Everyone who was anyone was out at Seven Oaks Farm. But were they really there to enjoy the match, or to see what was going on *behind* the scenes?

If you weren't there, then you missed Bridgehampton Polo Club heir **Sebastian Hughes.** One has to wonder just how much Sebastian is paying the priceless **Julia** to remain his assistant. Or, is he paying her anything at all? Women have been known to be extremely dedicated to the men they love.

Speaking of loyal…Sebastian's good friend and business partner, **Richard Wells,** made his

first public appearance since his horribly nasty divorce. And Hampton high society didn't take long to pounce. He seems to be giving the ladies a wide berth, though we did see him eyeing a certain gorgeous woman on horseback. Does he know he's lusting after the hired help? That's a scandal just waiting to happen.

We can't wait to see what the rest of the summer is going to give us. As the weather heats up, the gossip is just going to get juicier.

KATHERINE GARBERA

is a strong believer in happily-ever-after. She's written more than thirty-five books and has been nominated for career achievement awards in series fantasy and series adventure from *RT Book Reviews*. Her books have appeared on the Waldenbooks/Borders bestseller list for series romance and on the *USA TODAY* extended bestseller list. Visit Katherine on the Web at www.katherinegarbera.com.

YVONNE LINDSAY

New Zealand–born to Dutch immigrant parents, Yvonne Lindsay became an avid romance reader at the age of thirteen. Now married to her "blind date" and with two surprisingly amenable teenagers, she remains a firm believer in the power of romance. Yvonne feels privileged to be able to bring to her readers the stories of her heart. In her spare time, when not writing, she can be found with her nose firmly in a book, reliving the power of love in all walks of life. She can be contacted via her Web site, www.yvonnelindsay.com.

KATHERINE GARBERA

&

YVONNE LINDSAY

SECRETS, LIES...AND SEDUCTION

11-0606

Published by Silhouette Books
America's Publisher of Contemporary Romance

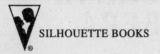 SILHOUETTE BOOKS

ISBN-13: 978-0-373-73032-2

Recycling programs
for this product may
not exist in your area.

SECRETS, LIES...AND SEDUCTION

Copyright © 2010 by Harlequin Books S.A.

The publisher acknowledges the copyright holders of the
individual works as follows:

CEO'S SUMMER SEDUCTION
Copyright © 2010 by Harlequin Books S.A.
Katherine Garbera is acknowledged as the author of
"CEO's Summer Seduction"

MAGNATE'S MISTRESS-FOR-A-MONTH
Copyright © 2010 by Harlequin Books S.A.
Yvonne Lindsay is acknowledged as the author of
"Magnate's Mistress-for-a-Month"

This edition published by arrangement with Harlequin Books S.A.

For questions and comments about the quality of this book please contact us
at Customer_eCare@Harlequin.ca.

® and TM are trademarks of Harlequin Books S.A., used under license.
Trademarks indicated with ® are registered in the United States Patent
and Trademark Office, the Canadian Trade Marks Office and in other
countries.

Visit Silhouette Books at www.eHarlequin.com

Printed in U.S.A.

CONTENTS

Dear Reader,

There's nothing like a warm summer night to spark high-stakes romance! From June through August 2010, Silhouette Desire is launching a new continuity miniseries—six romance-packed stories in three volumes. Escape with us to the glamorous celebrity playground of the Hamptons in A SUMMER FOR SCANDAL.

This month two stellar authors—*USA TODAY* bestseller Katherine Garbera and Yvonne Lindsay—contribute sassy stories to our *Secrets, Lies...and Seduction* (#2019) anthology, the first in the miniseries.

In July, *New York Times* and *USA TODAY* bestselling author Brenda Jackson teams up with Olivia Gates for the second installment, *In Too Deep* (#2025). And *USA TODAY* bestselling author Catherine Mann and Emily McKay end the miniseries with *Winning It All* (#2031). In August.

These romances are the perfect summer getaway— powerful, passionate and provocative!

Happy reading!

Krista Stroever

Senior Editor

CEO'S SUMMER SEDUCTION

KATHERINE GARBERA

To my new Soma friends for making me feel so welcome
in their store and being a heck of a lot of fun!

One

Julia Fitzgerald glanced at the Cartier diamond-encrusted watch on her wrist and then back at her notepad. Her boss would be here in exactly thirty seconds. Sebastian Hughes was prompt—he'd said more than once that time was money, and even though he had more of the green stuff than Midas, he still didn't like to waste it.

The Cartier was a constant reminder of why she skipped family celebrations and nights out with the girls—why she put up with such a demanding boss. Sebastian paid her very well to be his girl Friday.

The Seven Oaks Farm was a sprawling green farm with large horse paddocks and barns spread out. Right now it was quiet, but starting tonight it would become the epicenter of high society for the polo season.

"Julia, walk with me," Sebastian said as he strode

toward her. "I need to go down to the stables and check on the horses."

She nodded. She wore a pair of brown pumps with a nice square heel, ideal for traipsing all over the grounds—something that she knew Sebastian would want to do, since they only had two days before the opening of this year's polo season. And the Hugheses were the founders of the Bridgehampton Polo Club.

The polo club was actually an "in residence" club at the farm. Sebastian's family owned the farm with its two large houses and an apartment house that the sheikh had leased for the season for his grooms. She and Seb used his home office as their base of operations.

"This is where I want the tailgating tents set up. Bobby Flay is going to come down here to do one of his throwdowns with Marc Ambrose, our head chef. That will get us some great publicity for the opening. Please make sure that you have every detail of that ironed out."

"No problem," she said, tucking a strand of her long brown hair behind her ear.

Sebastian stopped and looked out over the grounds. He was tall and lanky and had a bit of five o'clock shadow on his jaw. He had a thick head of stylishly rumpled hair, which made him look like he'd just come from the arms of his latest lover.

"That's one thing I like about you, Jules."

"What? That I never say no?"

She spoke in a teasing tone because she knew that was what he expected. But to be honest she was a little annoyed. He called her Jules, even though she preferred to go by Julia. It sounded like a little thing, but she'd spent the first year she'd worked for Sebastian reminding him time and again that she went by Julia.

But it didn't matter. He was Sebastian Hughes, used to getting his own way in all things and intent on calling her Jules. And she was used to her salary.

"Exactly. You never say no," he said with that wide, sexy grin of his.

She hated that she found him attractive. Of course she'd have to be dead not to. He was tall, dark and rakishly handsome—a potent combination.

"Have you touched base with the gossip sites and the papers?"

"Yes. I've been working the phone night and day, making sure we have enough celebrities for them to cover. And rumor has it that Carmen Akins is coming this year. Since her divorce from Matthew Birmingham she is the paps' favorite target. That should guarantee us some extra coverage."

"Stay on it. Coverage is money, as far as this set is concerned. If no one knows they're here, they don't have a reason to come."

"I know," she said.

"After we check out the stables, I need you to run by the rehab home and update my father on our plans."

"Not a problem," Julia said. She actually liked visiting Sebastian's father at the rehab facility for people who were still recovering from chemo and cancer. Christian Hughes was a ladies' man who knew how to pour on the charm. She knew that Sebastian had the same skills, but they had never been directed at her since she worked for him.

Her BlackBerry twittered, and she glanced down at the screen. "Richard is driving up from the city. I've made sure the guesthouse is ready for him, stocked with all his favorite foods and drinks."

"Good. It's important that you see to Richard's

every need. I want him to have a carefree summer. He's stressed out due to that divorce of his."

"You're concerned about Richard's stress level?" she asked.

"It impacts our business. He needs to relax so he can start being engaged at work again."

Richard Wells was not only Sebastian's good friend but also his business partner—they had established the very successful Clearwater Media together. Julia knew Richard's divorce had more than shaken him. It had made him into someone different.

"I will do my best to make sure he enjoys his time here."

"That's all I ask," Sebastian said. "Have you heard from Sheikh Adham Aal Ferjani?"

"His flight is en route. I have confirmed he will be arriving at the heliport. I know you wanted to meet him, but he'll be landing about the same time as Richard."

Sebastian pulled out his BlackBerry and glanced at the screen. "I'll have drinks with Richard later. I will meet the sheikh. Or maybe I can send Vanessa."

"I'll be happy to call her," Julia said.

"Not necessary. I don't know if she can handle the sheikh, actually. What else do I have tonight?"

"Dinner with Cici."

Cici O'Neal was the heiress to the Morton Mansions luxury hotel chain and Sebastian's latest arm candy. She was actually a first-class pain. She called Julia almost every day with a new list of must-haves for her attendance at the polo season.

"I have one more thing I need you to do for me, Jules."

She glanced up from her big, leather-bound day planner into those crystal-blue eyes of his and wondered if he realized that she was on the edge of losing it. Maybe it was because he kept calling her Jules or maybe it was the fact that she was going to have to deal with Cici once again—she couldn't say for certain. She only knew that she was about to go ballistic, and that wasn't like her. She took a deep breath, but yoga breathing wasn't going to help. She was tired of being paid well to be invisible. She doubted Sebastian noticed that she kept her emotions carefully buttoned up. And he didn't pay her much attention anyway.

"Anything," she said with a forced smile.

Out of the corner of her eye she saw the sexy Argentine polo player Nicolas Valera riding out with the team. He was a ridiculously skilled polo player. Rumor had it that when he stopped playing he was going to model for Polo by Ralph Lauren.

"I need you to call Cici and tell her that things are over between us."

"What?" she asked, certain she'd misunderstood him because she'd let Nicholas distract her.

"Call Cici. After you speak to her, send her this," Sebastian said, removing a blue Tiffany's box from his pocket and handing it to her.

Julia automatically took the box before realizing what she was agreeing to do. She wasn't about to call his latest fling and break up with the woman for him. No matter how big a pain Cici was, she deserved to get the news from Sebastian himself.

Julia pushed the Tiffany's box back into his hands. She shook her head. "Absolutely not, Sebastian. You're going to have to take care of that yourself."

Sebastian blinked at his assistant. Jules never said no. At least not to him. He wasn't used to being denied anything. Ever. From anyone. He had learned early that if he acted like a man who always got his way then he did.

"I said no. I'm not going to break up with her for you. A private discussion between the two of you is what is needed."

"I'll decide what is needed. Cici knows we're not serious. This gift will ease any discomfort she might have."

Jules shook her head. "Cici has been calling every day with requests for the entire season here. That sounds serious to me. I'm not doing it. It's the most personal thing you've ever asked me to do—too personal."

"Visiting my father is personal. You have no problem with that," he said. "I don't have time for this, Jules."

"How many times have I asked you to call me Julia? You never listen to me."

"Hey, hold on here. I'm not sure where this is coming from. I thought we settled the nickname thing."

She gave him a sardonic smile. "No, *we* didn't. I just stopped mentioning it when it became clear you were never going to hear me."

Sebastian looked closely at Julia, possibly for the first time since he'd hired her two years ago. She was very attractive with long, silky brown hair hanging around her shoulders and deep chocolate eyes. He had realized when he interviewed her that he was attracted to her. But he knew he would never act on it. Men who slept with their assistants ended up looking like asses in business. And Sebastian was no one's fool. So he put the feelings aside.

But today, with the summer sun shining down on her, he was struck again by how pretty she was wearing a slinky sundress that left her muscled arms bare. With her sunglasses pushed to the top of her head and her eyes glaring up at him, however, she was more than just pretty—she was mad. He knew he was in trouble.

It wasn't anything he couldn't handle or easily rectify. Perhaps if he offered her a big enough bonus, she'd cave and do his dirty work.

"Let's talk, Jules—Julia," he said. He'd thought the nickname was fine, but he saw now that it really got to her. Or maybe it was the fact that he hadn't listened to her. Perhaps he should have.

"You can call Cici. I will make arrangements to deliver her gift," she said.

"I will make it worth your time to talk to Cici for me," he said. He didn't want to have to deal with Cici today. If they'd had a deeper relationship he would never have asked Julia to do this. But Cici was going out with him only because of his connections and standing. He liked the way she looked on his arm, but he had too many details to take care of this season. He'd expected—hell, they'd all expected—his dad to be back at the helm this year. But pancreatic cancer was taking longer to battle than Sebastian and his father had anticipated. His younger sister, Vanessa, said it was because Dad was used to getting his way in all things. So when Christian had told the doctors he needed to be back in his office by May, they'd all expected it would happen.

"Sebastian, are you listening to me? You can't make it worth my while. You're just going to have to talk to her yourself."

Underneath her tough-as-nails exterior, Julia had a soft heart. She was always trying to tell him what the women in his life wanted from him, like little romantic gestures that he imagined his assistant wanted from the men in her life.

"I will give you and your family an all-expenses paid vacation to Capri if you do this." He didn't know her family; he just assumed she had some and she'd like to spend time with them.

"Liar."

"What?"

"You won't let me have that vacation. My parents will be there enjoying Capri, and I'll be on my BlackBerry doing things for you."

"Fair enough," he said. "But how can I function without you, Jules, I mean, Julia. You are my right-hand gal."

"I know that. And you know I'll do just about anything you ask. But I'm not breaking up with Cici for you, Sebby."

"Sebby?"

"Why not? You keep calling me Jules."

He sighed, noting the gleam of amusement in her eyes. "I'm willing to give you fifty thousand dollars to do this."

The gleam of amusement changed to a look of pure anger, which took him aback.

"I thought we were negotiating," he said.

"No, we're not. I refuse to break up with a woman for you. That's a line I won't cross. Visiting your sick father, holding the hand of your divorced partner, keeping tabs on your wild sister—these things fit into my very broad job description. But breaking up with a woman? I won't do it."

"I'll double my offer," he said.

Julia looked stunned for a second. "You know what? I quit. I should have a long time ago. I keep telling myself that hard work will get me what I want, but I just can't do this anymore."

"Julia, you can't quit right as the polo season is starting. You know I need you, and you have me at your mercy."

"Do I? Or is this just another one of your games to get me to do what you want?"

"I do need you," he said sincerely. There was no way he could replace her and get the new person up to speed before the games started. He needed Jules by his side, taking care of the details he couldn't attend to.

"I want to believe that, but you'd say anything to keep me here now."

"Of course I would. I'll take care of Cici, and then we can go back to the way things were," he said.

She shook her head. "We can't. You think I'd do anything for money."

"You've just proven you won't," he said. "If you stay with me through the polo season, I will double your last month's salary and make sure you get a job at Clearwater where you are the boss. You can call the shots from now on. How does that sound?" he asked.

She tipped her head to the side and the breeze blew across the polo field, stirring her hair as they stood near the stables. He saw on her face that she wanted to believe him.

"I'm a man of my word. You know that."

She nodded. "It's a deal. But you have to break up with Cici."

"I already said I would," he reminded her.

She stuck her hand out. "Shake on it."

He did, feeling a little tingle go up his arm. Dammit, he didn't need to be reminded of his attraction to her right now. Her spark of temper and the way she'd stuck to her guns had kicked things up a notch.

"We have a deal, Julia," he said, holding on to her hand longer than he should have.

Julia didn't know what to make of Sebastian's latest offer. But he smiled smugly at her, making her feel like he'd gotten the better of her once again. She glanced at the Cartier watch on her wrist. Apparently she had a price after all. But then she'd grown up in a world far removed from the Hamptons and organizations like the Bridgehampton Polo Club. In fact, she'd never even realized what a big event polo could be until she'd taken this job with Sebastian.

He'd introduced her to a world that was beyond what she'd come to expect during her small-town Texas upbringing. And that world was one she'd always dreamed of.

"I'm going to visit Christian now," she said, pulling her hand out of his strong grasp, trying to ignore the little shiver that ran through her at his touch.

"Sounds good. I need to talk to Vanessa, and then I'll take care of Cici," Sebastian said.

"Later, I'm sampling the menu for our Black and White pre-opening night dinner. I want to make sure we don't have any hiccups." She turned to walk away.

"Jules."

"Yes?"

"Thank you for staying," he said.

He reached out and touched her shoulder, gazing at her with gorgeous blue eyes.

She could hardly think. After two years of being nothing but his girl Friday, she was suddenly very aware of him as a man—and that was dangerous. She didn't want to be attracted to Sebastian Hughes. He wasn't the kind of man who would give her what she needed in a boyfriend. He was more of a wild, hot fling.

Hadn't she seen enough of his dating roadkill to know that?

She nodded. "It was the professional thing to do."

"And you are always very professional."

"I try." This entire day was backfiring on her, and she was losing control of the situation. She stepped back from Sebastian, and his hand slid down her arm.

She almost gasped at the feel of his big, warm hand on her bare skin. He'd never really touched her before. Now she was glad of that—she would have been a mess in the office if he'd been like this when she'd first started.

"I don't think you should…" She struggled to finish the sentence.

"You have very soft skin," he said, stroking her arm.

"I use a moisturizer every day," she said, realizing how inane that sounded.

"I know. Peaches, right?"

"Yes," she said, heat rising to her face. How did he know that?

He rubbed his forefinger at the juncture inside her elbow, and she shivered with awareness. The ripple of his touch spread up her arm and down her chest to her breasts. She felt herself swell—her nipples tingled. She wanted to know what his touch would feel like on other parts of her body.

She shook her head, trying to force herself to stop feeling this attraction to him. To Sebastian Hughes. Her boss.

"I'm your assistant," she said, stepping back from him and pulling her arm from his hand. She wrapped it around her waist, then realized she was broadcasting vulnerability and dropped it to her side.

"For one more season. But I think my rule about no office romances is going to be bent."

"I have no intention of helping you bend that rule, Sebastian."

He leaned in closer, and the scent of his aftershave assailed her. He was taller than she was, and he blocked out the midafternoon sun that shone down on them. "Your eyes tell a different story when they linger on my face and my lips."

She felt her eyes widen. He knew she had lusted after him. So? She was human, and he was a very good-looking man. But he was her boss. And girls that slept with their bosses had notoriously short careers. "No."

He smiled. "We aren't going to be working together for much longer, Julia."

She shook her head. "Sebastian, I'm not an acquisition. You can't just insist that I do whatever you say. And I'm not going to change my mind simply because you won't take no for an answer," she said.

"Yes, you will."

Why was he so confident that he could have her? She thought she'd done a very good job of burying her attraction to him, but apparently it had not escaped his notice. Had he just been waiting for the right moment to take advantage of it?

No. It was too easy to accept Sebastian's public persona as his real personality. Underneath the born-with-a-silver-spoon exterior was the heart of a man who was a good friend, a loving son and brother and a good boss, no matter how demanding he was.

But what exactly was he demanding now?

"Mr. Hughes?"

Sebastian turned to greet the man who was coming across the field, and Julia took the opportunity to disappear. She wasn't sure what had just happened, but she knew she needed to get away from Sebastian Hughes. Quickly.

She made her way back to the office and sat down at her desk. In front of her computer, she regained her equilibrium. At least here she was in control and knew what was expected of her.

She confirmed with Chef Ambrose that he would have the sample menu ready for her to evaluate tonight at 7:00 p.m. Then she took care of a few last-minute details before getting ready to visit Christian.

She pushed the conversation with Sebastian to the back of her mind, shoving her response to his touch deep down into a box and locking it away. She was close to having what she wanted—Sebastian had promised to help her get a position in which she called the shots. She wanted to be in charge. She'd had enough of taking orders and was ready to be the boss.

She wasn't about to mess that up now.

She walked to her Volkswagen Bug convertible and got behind the wheel. It was a nice July day, and though it was hot, the heat wasn't as bad here as it was in her native Texas. She put the top down, tied a brightly colored scarf around her hair and put on her sunglasses.

With a new job, she might be able to afford that Audi A3 convertible that she'd had her eye on. She wouldn't be working with Sebastian, and that was for the best. He was a complicated man and made her life more complicated just by being in it. Should she have walked away?

It would have been hard, because she cared about the

Hughes family. Sebastian; his father, Christian; and his little sister, Vanessa, had all become a big part of her life and walking away…well, she wasn't ready to do that just yet. She had started over once, and doing so again now wasn't in her plans. Her plans, she thought. It would be best if she just remembered that she'd stayed because she wanted to.

She wasn't about to start over again, not now that she was close to having everything she'd always said she wanted. More money, a chance to be her own boss and Sebastian Hughes.

Whoa! She didn't want Sebastian!

She shook her head.

Yes, she did. And knowing she was here for only one more season was going to make him hard to resist.

Two

Christian Hughes was a smooth talker. Julia could hear the sound of his deep voice as she walked down the hall to his room. His private nurse, Lola, smiled at Julia as they passed each other in the hall.

"How is he today?" Julia asked.

"Full of himself," Lola said.

She'd tried to visit Christian yesterday but when she'd arrived, he'd already gone to sleep. So she'd come bright and early this morning with his favorite pastry—a chocolate-chip brioche—by way of apology.

She walked around the corner with a smile on her face. "Good morning, Christian."

"Ah, Julia, always a reason to have a good morning when you are visiting."

She smiled down at him. Christian waved the attendant from the room as Julia came to sit in the chair next to the bed. His head was shaved and he wore a dressing gown of deep navy blue, which made his own blue eyes seem brighter. In his lapel he had tucked a small rose, and he looked dapper and gentlemanly.

He had a breakfast tray next to his bed, and she shifted it into place. The rehab center where Christian was convalescing as he recovered from his latest round of chemo catered to a very wealthy crowd, so his private room scarcely resembled a hospital room. It had marble floors and a Moroccan rug that, according to Christian, Vanessa had purchased for him. There were photos on the wall of Vanessa and Sebastian, plus a few framed prints of past polo champion teams.

Seven Oaks Farm and the polo club were Christian's pride and joy, just as his children were.

"Sorry I didn't get to visit with you yesterday," she said. She took the bouquet she'd picked up at the grocery store out of her large Coach bag and changed the flowers next to his bedside table.

"I understand. Did the sheikh arrive yesterday?"

"He did. Sebastian made sure he was welcomed. His prized ponies are in the stables."

"Have you seen them yet?" Christian asked.

"No, not yet. I'm hoping to get down there today."

"If they are anything like their sire, I think you will be impressed. I'll look forward to hearing about them," Christian said.

Julia made a mental note to bring pictures of the horses when she came back. Everyone had expected Christian to have recovered in time for this season but it was just not going to happen.

"I'll give you a full report," Julia assured him. Then she launched into the specifics of the Black and White event that they were hosting as a preopening party. The details were coming together. Christian asked lots of questions, as she'd expected him to, and he made a few suggestions. When she glanced at her watch, she realized that more than an hour had passed.

He saw her check the time and sighed. "I suppose you have to be going."

"I do. Your son is a very demanding boss."

"I guess that's trying," he said.

"Not at all. He reminds me a lot of you," she said. "I know it takes determination and drive to be successful in life."

"That's true. I tried to raise him right."

"I think you did. Was your wife as driven as you are?" she asked. Julia knew little of Sebastian's mother, Lynette, other than that she'd died in a car accident five years earlier.

"Lynette was a very good wife for me and understood the importance of position," Christian said.

Julia sensed there was more to Lynette than Christian was saying but she appreciated the fact that he wasn't going to gossip about his deceased wife.

"I'll stop by tomorrow," Julia said, standing. She made a note to see when Vanessa would be visiting her father. Julia always tried to time her visits when she knew Christian would be alone. Though she had no close family, she knew it was important that she not intrude on his children's time with him.

"I will look forward to it."

"What will you look forward to, Dad?" Sebastian said, entering the room. He smiled at her and went to give his dad a hug. Julia stood back to give him room. Her gaze lingered on Sebastian, and she had to force herself to look away.

Seeing this side of her boss always unnerved her. In the office he was demanding and could even be ruthless.

But here his guard was down, and she saw the man as a loving, devoted son.

"Seeing Julia," Christian said.

"We all look forward to that," Sebastian said. "Did she tell you that she almost quit on me?"

"No. What did you do?" Christian asked.

"Why do you assume I did something?" Sebastian asked with an easy grin. He winked at her, and she felt a twinge of sexual awareness. It didn't help that she'd dreamed of him last night.

"I *am* your father, Seb."

"True enough. Did Julia catch you up on all of the details for the Black and White event?"

"She did. But I want to hear about Sheikh Adham Aal Ferjani's ponies. Did you see them?"

"I'm going to let you two chat," Julia said.

"Dad, I'll be right back. I need to speak to Julia alone for a minute."

"Take your time," Christian said.

Julia walked out of the room with Sebastian at her side. He led the way down the hall to the sitting room for the visiting families. She took her notepad from her bag so she could take notes, but Sebastian put his hand on hers and shook his head.

"Thank you."

"For what?"

"For not letting yesterday affect the way you deal with my dad."

"I like him."

"Good. He likes you, too. So we're okay now?"

"Yes," she said. "I'm not holding on to any anger from yesterday."

"You were angry?" he asked.

She playfully punched him in the arm, trying to

maintain the relationship they'd always had, but things were changing between them. Sebastian had never thanked her for doing this type of thing before and she couldn't help but think that he was starting to see her in a different way.

"I think you know I was," she said.

"I do," he said, leaning closer to her. The scent of his aftershave made her very aware of him as a man. He was ratcheting up the charm, she thought. She'd seen him act this way before with other women, but somehow this felt different.

"Julia, we didn't get to finish our conversation," he said.

"Which one?"

"About breaking the rules of office romances."

Julia took a deep breath. "I've got work to do and we are done with that conversation."

He stared deep into her eyes and she caught her breath. "Do you really mean that?"

"Yes, I do," she said, but she knew it was a lie. *Oh, my God,* she thought, *Sebastian Hughes has turned me into a liar.* She turned on her heel and fled down the hall before she decided to confess all and give Sebastian carte blanche to her heart.

Sebastian stayed with his father until Vanessa arrived. Christian was much healthier now than he had been two months earlier, but he and Vanessa were still worried about him. They'd never been close to their mother, who had cared more about her position in Hamptons society than about her children. Their father had been their rock.

When he got back to Bridgehampton and Seven Oaks Farm, he found a neatly written note from Julia on his desk in the main house. The scent of her lingered in his office. He was going to miss working with her every day. But if he had his way, he would be getting to know her much better before she left at the end of the season. And who knew what that might lead to?

He suddenly realized he needed to be very careful. Emotional connections could be the downfall of a successful man. Richard was a perfect example of that. His friend's divorce had shaken him and left him devastated. He no longer functioned the way he used to. Sebastian couldn't afford to let something like that happen to him. Maybe he should back off a bit.

He heard footsteps on the Italian marble floor outside his office, and then Julia walked in. "Oh, you're back."

"Indeed, I am."

"I'm going to talk to Chef Ambrose. He is doing a caviar and white truffle hors d'oeuvre for the Black and White event. And last night's didn't taste right. I wanted your opinion on it," she said, sounding completely businesslike.

"I'll come with you," he said, standing. "I only have a few minutes before I head over to the training field. I know that the sheikh's horses will be worked out this morning, and I want to see them in action."

"Me, too," she admitted. "I've heard so much about them. Your father is jealous he can't be here for the event."

"I'm working on that," Sebastian said as they walked. "I'd like to try to get him here for the opening match."

"I will talk to Lola when I get back to the office and see what she thinks about that."

"Good. Please call Dr. Gold and get his opinion."

"I will do that."

They'd reached the main kitchens. Even though it was midmorning, they were already busy. The Seven Oaks Farm had a first-class chef, and the kitchens were always available for their guests and club members.

"Chef Ambrose asked that you wait for him in the kitchen," Jeff said. Jeff was Ambrose's saucier and was a valuable asset.

"Thank you, Jeff." Sebastian led the way.

Julia stood off to one side making notes in her leather-bound planner. The sun shone through the small window, making her dark hair shine. She tipped her head to the side, and he realized again what a beautiful woman she was. Not because she was an asset to his office but because she was a woman. He saw beyond his ultraefficient, never-says-no assistant to...Julia.

"Why are you staring at me?" she asked.

"You're very pretty," he said. Then he realized he sounded like an idiot.

She laughed. "Thanks. Are you just now noticing?"

"I guess I am. I've always thought you were pleasing to look at. But this is different."

She arched one eyebrow. "How so?"

He shrugged. "I'm not sure. But—"

"Sebastian...I don't think—"

He figured she'd say that. "Listen, I want you to know—"

"Sorry to keep you waiting, Seb," Marc Ambrose said. "I had to talk to the Food Network people for tomorrow's cooking event."

"It's not a problem. We didn't mind the wait. Now what do you have for us?" Sebastian asked.

Julia had moved away from him and set down her

clipboard next to the plate that Marc indicated she should taste first.

He knew it was a bad idea to be attracted to his assistant. But he had promised to help her move on, and in his mind, that meant they weren't working together for that much longer. She was no longer off-limits to him.

And knowing that had changed the way he saw her. But he knew she might not feel the same way. He was a demanding boss, and he often saw the telltale signs of her irritation with him. But she always held her tongue and did what he asked.

That had been enough for him before, but now...now he wanted more. He wanted to see those pretty eyes of hers watching him with desire. He wanted her to want him.

He had never been a man to accept no for an answer, and he wasn't going to start with Julia now. But perhaps he was going about this all wrong. Clearly Julia knew him very well—better than most—and wouldn't be swayed by his usual tactics. He was going to have to get real with her. And stop ordering her around like a regular employee. It was time to step up his game.

She glanced at him and mouthed the word *what?* He waited until Marc left the room to get the next plate and walked over to her.

"We are having dinner together tonight," he said.

"At the VIP Black and White event, yes, I know."

"I want you by my side tonight." Apparently it wasn't as easy to stop issuing her orders as he'd thought.

"Why?" she asked. "I think we should cover different sides of the room."

He shook his head. "Not this year. This year you will be with me. I'd like you by my side."

Surprise registered in her dark eyes, and she gave a quick nod as the chef brought them another plate.

Julia's day was very busy, which was good—it kept her from feeling nervous about the dinner. What had gotten into Sebastian? Why had he asked her to join him tonight in such a…formal way? She tried to shake off the anxiety and focus. She looked at her to-do list as she sat in her office. She still had to get down to the stables and take pictures of the sheikh's horses to show Christian tomorrow.

It was almost four-thirty, and she had to go to the house she was staying in to get changed before tonight's dinner. She grabbed her digital camera and headed down to the stables, where she ran into Richard walking back toward the guesthouse. He was a good-looking man, but the events of the last few months weighed on him.

She knew Sebastian was hoping that this month spent at Seven Oaks would relax Richard and help him find his way back to the man he used to be.

"Julia," Richard said.

"Are you enjoying yourself, Richard?" she asked. Though Richard and Sebastian were partners, she didn't work closely enough with Richard to feel comfortable asking him anything more personal than that.

"I am. I spent the morning watching the grooms practice with the polo ponies."

"Are the sheikh's horses as impressive as I've heard?" she asked.

"They are," Richard said. She noticed that he had a far-off look in his eyes, and she wondered if perhaps there was more going on with him than just recovering from his recent divorce.

"Good. I promised Christian a full report on them," she said, holding up her camera.

"I bet you could ask the trainer to talk to Christian via videoconference," Richard said.

"What a great idea. That way he'll feel like he's here even though he can't leave his room. Thanks, Richard."

"No problem. Christian is a great guy. The kind of father I wish I had."

"Don't we all. Sebastian is one lucky man."

"Yes," Richard said, "he is."

Richard left, walking back toward the main building, and Julia continued down toward the stables. Why hadn't she thought of the videoconference idea? It was fantastic. She quickly called Lola and asked if they could set up a computer monitor in Christian's room.

When she arrived in the stables, she saw Catherine Lawson, the sheikh's head groom. "Ms. Lawson?"

"Yes?"

"I'm Julia Fitzgerald, Sebastian Hughes's assistant."

"Nice to meet you. Are you here to see the ponies?"

"I am. I'd also like to ask a favor."

"I can't let you ride them," she said with a grin.

Julia laughed. "Thank God. I'd probably fall off and break my neck."

Catherine laughed, too. "What can I do for you?"

"Sebastian's dad started the Bridgehampton Polo Club and is a huge polo fan, but he can't come to the matches. I was wondering if you'd mind letting me take some photos and maybe a video of you with the horses so he could see them."

"I don't mind at all," Catherine said.

"Great." Julia talked to Catherine for the next hour, spending longer than she'd meant to at the stables. She got the photos and video she wanted, and set up a time for the videoconference.

She got back to the office with no time to spare and found Sebastian waiting for her. "I'm meeting Richard for a game of tennis in the morning. Would you please add that to my schedule?"

"I will."

"Tonight, Carmen Akins is coming to the Star Room. If you could be there when she arrives and make sure that every detail is taken care of, that would be great. We want to make the most of having her here."

"I'm on it. I need thirty minutes to run home and change, and then I'll be back here."

"I'll pick you up," Sebastian said. "We have a date tonight."

"A work function," she replied, trying to not make it seem so intimate. But she knew it was too late. She was going out with Sebastian tonight and she wanted to make sure she looked her best.

"It's a date," Sebastian said. "And later on we will stop by the Star Room and check out the local scene."

"I'm not sure—"

"I am."

She sighed. Sebastian was making it very hard for her to keep up the wall she wanted between them.

"Vanessa mentioned you had Dad talk to Catherine Lawson via a videoconference. That was brilliant."

She blushed at his praise. "It was Richard's suggestion."

"He's a good friend, but you pulled it together."

"Richard seems to be enjoying his time out here," Julia said, not wanting the praise that Sebastian was giving her.

"He is. If you can find time on the calendar for next week, let's see if the three of us can sit down and talk about your new role within our organization."

She nodded. She had made a note to bring up that very topic but hadn't had a chance to. She'd never doubted that Sebastian would follow through on what he'd said. She was glad that he was moving forward with it, but a part of her was going to miss this job and Sebastian.

"Anything else?" she asked.

"Yes. My dad really enjoyed the videoconference. Thank you, Julia."

She shook her head. "I was just doing my job."

"You did a lot more than that."

She needed to change the conversation—he was making her wish that she could keep working for him. But she knew that would never happen. He wouldn't be treating her the way he was now if she wasn't leaving. *Remember that,* she thought.

She left his office without a backward glance, before he could say anything else. Her mind should have been full of all the tasks she still had to accomplish before the end of the evening, but instead she could think only of Sebastian, of the new way he was speaking to her and looking at her. Just yesterday he'd been hitting on her mercilessly. Now he was behaving like a gentleman—almost.

Was he trying to convince her he could be serious about her?

Could she handle it if he was?

Sebastian Hughes was so far out of her league that

she hardly even knew how to process the thought. He was so shockingly wealthy, and she was…not. How would people respond if they were a couple? Would the relationship last?

Or would she just end up with a phone call from his new assistant and a blue box from Tiffany's?

Three

It was almost eleven o'clock, and the Star Room was busy and noisy—exactly the kind of atmosphere they needed. The local jet set was in attendance, as well as celebrities who'd either come up from the city for the weekend or flown out from the West coast.

All in all Sebastian was pleased by what he saw. The Bridgehampton Polo Club was still a draw and he was glad to know that the VIPs would still turn up, even if he was at the helm and not his father.

He spotted Julia standing near the bar talking to Catherine Lawson. Both women seemed out of place in the nightclub but for different reasons. Despite the martini in her hand, Julia looked like she was still working, and Catherine looked like she wanted to be back out in the stables.

Sebastian made his way through the room, taking the time to talk to everyone he saw. Working the room was important not just because it was the start of the season but because the Hughes family had always tried to make everyone who came for the opening feel at home.

When he was finally at Julia's side, she had finished her martini and was chatting with two young women he didn't recognize.

"Hello, Sebastian," Julia said as he approached.

"Evening, Julia, ladies." The women said their goodbyes to Julia and walked off. They were as alone as they could be in the crowded club.

Julia smiled at him. "Do you want a drink?"

"No. Just a word with you—in private."

"Good. I'm ready for my evening to be over," she said.

"I bet you are," he said. "Long day?"

"Yes, it has been. Shall we debrief?" she asked.

"Let's go outside."

"It's closed tonight," she said.

"Not for me."

"I forgot who I was with."

"Did you?"

"Only for a minute," she said. "I'm going to miss this next year."

"You'll still be invited next year," he said. "You are a valuable part of the Clearwater family."

She nodded. She meant she'd miss being with him. And that was the truth, she thought. It didn't matter that she'd tried to pretend she was working tonight—she'd enjoyed herself at dinner. Had liked being at Sebastian's side as his hostess, and that was the job she really wanted. But Sebastian was dangerous. She had to be careful not to let him seduce her into falling for him. He was a player and he would move on.

Sebastian led the way out of the Star Room. He didn't

want to think about Julia not being here with him next year. Even though he'd given his word to help her find another job—a position where she could be in charge and not have to answer directly to him—he wanted her by his side.

"I've been thinking about your new job."

"What about it?" she asked. "Did you change your mind?"

"Not at all. You know I'm a man of my word."

"I do know that. I'm just afraid that…well, that something will come up and I won't get a good position within Clearwater."

Sebastian shook his head. "Not if I have anything to do with it. I want you to have what you've worked so hard for. That's important to me, Julia."

She glanced up at him. Her hair was pulled back in a loose chignon, making her features seem even more delicate than usual. In the moonlight, with the warm summer breeze stirring the air, she seemed ethereal. Like she didn't belong here with him. In fact, he knew she didn't. Julia Fitzgerald wasn't his kind of woman. Or rather, he wasn't her kind of man.

He knew she was too solid, too real for the come-and-go relationships he usually engaged in. She wasn't the kind of woman who would accept a piece of jewelry when things ended. And they would end. Because he couldn't be the man she deserved. But for some reason that wasn't enough to deter him. He still wanted her.

He closed the distance between them and caught a tendril of hair that had escaped from her updo. He twirled the long, silky length around his finger.

"Sebastian, as I tried to say earlier, this isn't a good time for this," she said. "I have thought of nothing else but my career since I came here. I don't want to lose my focus now."

"I know that, Julia, but I'm afraid that I can't ignore this any longer. There is something about you...."

"Are you saying I've mesmerized you?" she asked in that sardonic way she had.

"No. I'm saying that now that I've allowed myself to see you as a sexy woman, I can't get you out of my head."

"A sexy woman? I'm not that. Not at all."

"Yes, you are," he said. There was something innately sensual about Julia. He'd noticed from the very beginning, from the first time he'd interviewed her. She was simply someone who moved with a very feminine awareness of her body. She was at home with herself, and that made men appreciate her looks.

"I'm not prepared to be your latest fling," she said.

"I'm not asking you to be," he said.

"Then what is it you want, Sebastian?" she asked, looking up at him with confusion in her eyes.

She licked her lips, and he realized he knew exactly what he wanted. Her mouth under his and her curvy body pressed against him. He pulled her to him and lowered his head to take her mouth in a kiss that would change everything.

Julia hadn't meant to kiss Sebastian, or even let him kiss her, but once his mouth touched hers all bets were off. He tasted of the martini and something that was uniquely Sebastian. His mouth felt right against hers—exactly right.

Even his hands on her shoulders, drawing her closer into the curve of his body, felt right. He skimmed his hands down her bare arms and tangled his fingers with hers as his mouth roamed and his tongue plunged deeper, making her forget about everything except this balcony and this moment.

The summer wind stirred the hair at the nape of her neck, wrapping around them both. She let go of his hands and slipped her arms around Sebastian's lean waist, holding on to him as he deepened their embrace. His free hand roamed up and down her back, urging her closer to his body. She liked the feel of his muscled chest pressed against her.

He pulled back and dropped a couple of nibbling kisses against her lips. Then he opened his mouth over hers, and she felt the brush of his lips and the humid warmth of his breath. She shivered in response to his touch.

She felt wicked kissing him out here where the world could see. She'd never done anything the least bit untoward—and now she wanted to. With Sebastian, she wanted to be the woman she'd never had the courage to be.

She put a hand on the back of his neck and felt the smoothness and coolness of his hair against her fingers. She traced a line over his neck and down to his shoulder and then pulled back to look up at him. His eyes were half-closed, and in the moonlight she'd never seen anything sexier than this man.

She'd never felt as feminine and womanly as she did in his arms. It had never felt this intense with other lovers. The fire in her veins overpowered her and scared her. Suddenly, she didn't want to feel it anymore.

She jerked back from Sebastian, stumbling a little until she found her balance.

"That was interesting," Sebastian said.

"That was wrong. I work for you."

"Not for much longer."

"I'll still be working for you, even if not so directly. I can't do this, Seb...."

"Why not?"

"This is too intense for me. Our relationship works because I do my job and keep my head down. I don't want to start this."

"I don't think I can stop now that we've started, Julia."

She stared at him in the moonlight. His features were stark, and she saw the signs of desire in his eyes. He wanted her. Heck, she wanted him, too, but how was she going to work with him when she knew what it felt like to be in his arms?

This was a mistake. She should have quit when he'd asked her to break up with his girlfriend.

"Please stop overthinking this, Julia. We'll figure it out."

"How?"

"By not worrying about it. We're both adults. I know we can handle this."

"I don't want people to think of me as your latest fling." Not that she cared what other people thought, but what she felt right now was too intense to share with anyone.

"No one needs to know," he said. "It will be our business. I want it to develop naturally. I like kissing you and having you in my arms."

"I like it, too," she admitted. "But something doesn't feel right."

"What is it?" he asked.

"We're from two different worlds. Yours has money, mine doesn't. I can't exist in your world unless I'm working for you. And I don't think you'd know how to put a woman first if you tried."

Sebastian didn't say anything. She wondered for a moment if she'd said too much, but to be honest, she didn't care. She had to tell the truth, and if he walked away now, that was better than if she slept with him and fell for him and he walked away later.

She'd express-mailed enough Tiffany's boxes for Sebastian to have a very clear picture of just how often he changed women in his life.

"You deserve to come first, Julia. Every woman does," he said. "I'm not in a position to make you any promises about anything except that I want you and will make you a very happy woman while we are together."

Was that enough for her? Could she give in to her desire and just deal with the consequences later?

"I'm not sure—"

"Why not have a little fun?" he asked with that roguish grin of his. "We aren't going to be boss/assistant for much longer. You could use some fun, Julia—you work too hard."

He had a point. And she'd always wondered what it would be like to have a summer fling. She'd always been too serious to accept an offer like this before. And she'd certainly never received such an offer from a man like Sebastian Hughes.

"Okay," she said. "But please, Sebastian, remember who I am. I'm not Cici. I'm not a girl who wants to end up on the society page."

"I know what kind of girl you are." He pulled her into his arms again. "This is the kind of deal that needs to be sealed with a kiss."

He lowered his head, and this time she thought she was ready for the intensity of his kiss but she wasn't.

His touch was electric and made everything feminine in her react.

It was going to be one heck of a summer.

Sebastian wanted to take Julia home with him tonight. But he wasn't sure she was ready, so he glanced around the room.

"Do you mind staying a little longer?"

"No! I mean, that's fine with me."

He knew he'd read Julia right.

He watched Julia as she talked to Scott Markim, a professional basketball player, and his latest girlfriend. She handled herself with great ease for someone who claimed to feel out of place. Julia was the first woman he'd been with at an event like this who didn't constantly demand his attention. Julia did her own thing.

It was as if they were equals.

Of course they were equals. She'd probably smack him if she realized he'd thought something like that. But what he'd meant was she didn't need him to tell her where she belonged. Though this wasn't her social set, she blended in well here. During the last two years that she had worked for him, she'd picked up all the skills she needed to fit right in.

They had a deejay tonight but tomorrow night after the opening day polo match, they were going to have Brit pop sensation Steph Cordo performing live. Steph was the U.K.'s answer to Kelly Clarkson. She was young and had a voice that could wring emotion out of any lyric. And it had been a coup for them to get her to perform here. In their favor was that Steph was a Brit and she liked polo.

He spotted Vanessa working her way through the crowd with Nicolas Valera, and he watched her. Last year she'd had an affair with him, and it had ended badly with Vanessa acting out and giving the gossipmongers a lot to talk about.

Sebastian kept an eye on her because he didn't want a repeat of last year. He felt partially responsible for her behavior because their father had been sick, and Sebastian had taken on more duties, leaving Vanessa at loose ends.

She'd been easy prey for a playboy like Nicolas. Most of the polo players were treated like rock stars and had groupies. He never wanted Vanessa to be thought of as being in that crowd, though she had always been a wild child. He imagined that came from being the much-loved, very indulged younger sister.

When it was clear that their mother was not at all interested in her children, Sebastian had stepped in to make sure that Vanessa felt loved and never suffered from the cold shoulder that their mother offered. He knew it wasn't the same—a brother could never take the place of a mother—but he had tried.

"Enjoying the night?" he asked Vanessa as he dropped a kiss on her cheek.

"I am. Lots of fun people here tonight. You did a great job of getting exactly the right mix."

"Thank you," Sebastian said. "I think most of the credit should go to Julia. She worked the phone like nobody's business."

"She is an asset. I know Dad thinks she's part of the reason you've made the club even more successful."

"Part of the reason? He doesn't think it's just my charming way?" he teased her.

"You're the only one who thinks you are charming."

"I'm wounded."

"As if," she said. "What do you know about Nicolas Valera?"

"Nessa, you're not getting involved with him again."

Vanessa's face went white for a second. Then she groaned. "Stop being overprotective, Seb. I want to know if he's involved with anyone right now. Just curiosity."

"He hurt you," Sebastian said, wrapping his arm around her. "Stay away from him. You know he's not the man for you."

"I don't need your protection any longer," she said.

"I'll decide that."

"You are impossible," she said, and turned and walked away.

Sebastian took a sip of his soda water and watched his little sister walk away. He just wanted what was best for her. He didn't want to see her hurt again by Valera. And if she was talking about Valera, then that meant she was still interested in him.

"Still bossing your sister around?" Richard asked behind him.

"Always. I was going to come by your place for a drink in a little while."

"I needed some air, so I decided to put in an appearance after all."

"Are you doing okay?" Sebastian asked, leading the way to one of the banquettes at the edge of the room.

"I'm fine. I just don't want to spend too much time thinking, you know?"

Sebastian did know. After his mother's death, he'd analyzed that relationship up one side and down the other trying to figure out what he could have done differently. Could he have been a better son to her? Would that have changed the way she'd treated him?

In the end, he'd come to no conclusion except that he needed to stop thinking about it.

"I do. Have you been relaxing at all?"

"Had an early morning walk around the grounds and checked out the stables."

"There are lots of women here that can help you forget your troubles, Rich."

"I'm not ready for lots of women," his friend said.

"Fair enough. But don't let too much time pass."

"I'm not like you are, Seb, always moving on. I liked being married."

That was true, from what he'd observed. A part of Sebastian had always envied Richard's marriage and the fact that he had someone to go home to every night. But seeing the pain his friend had been in…that had convinced Sebastian the short-term affairs he was best suited to were better in the long run anyway.

He glanced up and saw Julia was looking at him. He wondered how he was going to say goodbye to her. He wanted her more than he had any of the other women he'd had in his life. But he knew he wasn't marriage material.

He knew he shouldn't be thinking of goodbye when they were just starting their affair, but remembering that this would end was important—he didn't want to end up like Richard.

Not that she'd even want him. She was a career-focused woman. Still, he wanted her. And he didn't want to have to think about why he did.

Four

Julia went to work the next day expecting things to be different, but in the office Sebastian was the same. He'd kissed her, talked her into an affair, and then backed off. She felt unsure and hated that.

He was hosting Geoff Devonshire, a schoolmate of his who was the son of Malcolm Devonshire, the billionaire entrepreneur, as well as a minor royal. So he was out of her hair for the day. She spent the bulk of the morning checking gossip Web sites and making sure that the polo club and Seven Oaks Farm were mentioned. It was important that the people who wanted to be talked about were, and the ones who wanted to keep their presence a secret did.

And Sebastian and Christian before him had prided themselves on giving their guests what they wanted.

Her phone rang, and she answered it without looking

at the caller ID. "Bridgehampton Polo Club, Sebastian Hughes's office, this is Julia."

"Jules, baby, how's it shaking?" Sebastian said.

She rolled her eyes. "I thought I said don't call me 'Jules.'"

"Now that we've kissed, I thought a nickname would be appropriate."

She shivered, remembering his mouth on hers. And the steamy dreams it had inspired last night. She hated to admit it, but "Jules" was growing on her. Perhaps it was because his voice softened the slightest bit when he called her by that nickname. "Fine. You can call me that when no one else is around."

He laughed. "You do remember I'm the boss, right?"

"Not in our off-hours."

"Are you going to order me around?" he asked. His voice dropped down to a low, husky tone that made her stomach flutter.

"Do you want me to?" she asked.

"Maybe. I prefer to be in charge, but if you need to be then we can talk about it," he replied. She could hear the grin in his voice.

"Did you call simply to give me a hard time?" she asked.

"Not at all. Listen, Geoff's wife is arriving at the heliport, and we can't break away from our round of golf. Would you pick her up?" Sebastian asked.

"What did I say about personal errands?" She was already putting her computer to sleep and getting her keys out.

"Believe it or not, this is polo club business. She's the heiress Amelia Munroe."

"Okay, I'll fetch her for you. Is she here low-key or should I let the media know?" Julia asked.

"I think low-key for right now. I'll give you the go-ahead when they want people to know she's here. They're staying in the guesthouse."

"Should I take her there?"

"No, bring her out to the stables. Geoff is going to take her riding."

"Anything else, boss?"

"Yes."

She waited, pen in hand so she could take notes.

"Thank you for taking that video over to Dad. He called me to tell me how great you are and warned me not to let you slip away. Did you set up another videoconference?"

"Yes, with Nicolas."

"Do you think that's wise?" Sebastian asked. But she ignored that. His affair with Vanessa had left tension between the two men.

She was touched that Christian had called to praise her. But she knew that no matter what his father said, Sebastian wasn't going to hold on to her. Not professionally—and not personally, either.

Suddenly she wanted to ask him some questions. She needed to figure out why Sebastian was always going through life—and women—at breakneck speed. Why didn't he want to put down roots the way his father had? What was it that made Sebastian the way he was? Of course, those were the very questions that would send a man like him running in the opposite direction.

"I didn't mind talking to your dad," she said, changing the topic from Nicolas. "I like your dad. He's funny and charming. How did that skip you?"

Sebastian laughed. "Thanks for agreeing to get

Amelia. Geoff is actually doing business on the golf course, and he didn't want her to be alone."

"I don't mind. I'll text you when we're on our way back."

"Thanks. You know, I've thought of nothing but our kiss last night and taking it further."

"Me, too," she confessed.

"Good."

She hung up and tidied her office area, which was really a sitting room attached to Sebastian's office. Her little Louis XIV desk was beautiful and she loved the large glass windows that looked out over the Seven Oaks Farm. From here she could see the paddocks where the horses were roaming. She could get used to this life.

She had to sign for a FedEx package, which she put on Sebastian's desk before leaving. She drove to the heliport to pick up the heiress and found that the paparazzi were already alerted to her presence.

Amelia smiled as she walked over to her, waving at the media. "Are you Jules?"

Julia nodded, knowing that Sebastian was having a bit of fun with her. "I am. And you're Amelia Munroe-Devonshire, right?"

"Too right," she said crisply. "Geoff's doing a deal right now?"

"That's what I heard, but he and Sebastian are on the golf course so it's anyone's guess what's going on."

"I know my husband. If he's not here, it must be business."

She smiled at Amelia's confidence. She was a woman very secure in her relationship, and Julia envied her that. She wished that she could be that confident in her relationship with Sebastian. But she knew when she'd agreed to date him what she was getting into. Had she made a mistake?

"I'm to take you to the farm. I think you attended our season two years ago, is that right?" Julia said as they got into her car and pulled away from the heliport. Julia had looked up Amelia and made sure she knew everything there was on the heiress.

"I did. It was a lot of fun. Christian Hughes is such a darling man. I didn't know that Geoff and Sebastian had been school chums until we were married."

Amelia kept Julia's mind off the fact that she was becoming more and more insecure about her decision by the minute. No matter what Sebastian said, she knew she didn't belong to the world of people like Amelia and Geoff Devonshire. Wouldn't Sebastian just get bored with her and go looking for someone who did belong? As she dropped Amelia off, she hesitated for a moment, wanting to join them. But in the end, she still felt like Sebastian's girl Friday, not his lover. And there was a good chance that would never change.

Sebastian watched Julia drive away, wishing she had stayed. But it would have been awkward to explain why he'd had his assistant come to dinner with them. And though Geoff was one of the most discreet men he knew, he sensed that he couldn't push things with Julia.

She seemed skittish about making their relationship public. And given his track record with women, he supposed he didn't blame her. But he wanted her around—he wanted to look at her, hear her laugh, touch her flawless skin. He missed her while he spent the evening with his friend and new wife. They were obviously in love and enjoyed being married.

He made an excuse to Geoff and Amelia and cut out

early. Not that the lovebirds would miss him. He drove to the guesthouse where Richard was staying, but his friend wasn't home. He didn't relish going back to an empty house. He wanted to see Julia. He couldn't deny it any longer. He needed to taste those lips again, to feel her perfect body pressed against his. He didn't want to wait.

He dialed her cell, and she answered on the first ring.

"Sebby, what's up?"

"Nothing, Jules. I was calling to see if you were free," he said.

"I am not."

"Got a date?" he asked. He didn't think she had time in her life to date anyone, and he knew Julia well enough to know that if there was a man in her life, she would have told him to shove off when he'd kissed her last night. Damn, was that only last night? It seemed like a lifetime had passed since he'd held her. He needed more—a lot more.

"I do have a date. With my DVR. I've been recording that new detective show with the crime writer and policewoman, and I'm dying to catch up."

"You'd rather watch TV than come out with me?"

"Sebastian, it's bad enough that I let you make me a workaholic. I need a night where I sit and stare at the wall to recover."

"Can I come help you recover?" he asked.

He turned his car around and headed toward Julia's place as she gave him a bunch of reasons why he shouldn't come over. She was just finishing as he pulled into the long driveway and drove up to the front of the house.

"Are you outside my door?" she asked.

"Yes, ma'am. Are you going to let me in?" he asked.

"Why aren't you partying with the Devonshires?" The front porch light came on and then her door opened.

"Because they're newlyweds and it was too…"

He hung up his phone without finishing his thought, pocketing it as he got out of the car. He walked toward her front door and took in the sight of her. She was gorgeous, and he couldn't wait to be with her. He didn't want to feel this way—not about Julia and not right now. But that didn't change the fact that he did.

"I suppose you think I'm going to let you in," she said.

They both knew she was going to. "I do indeed. And I'm hoping you have more of whatever it is you are drinking."

"I have an entire case. It's from the Grant Vineyards."

"Sabrina's family?"

"Yes. She sent a case to you, as well. It's at the office."

"I see you took the pinot noir," he said, knowing from past experience it was her favorite.

"I did," she said. They were quiet for a moment. She didn't step back and welcome him inside her house. "Sebastian, if I let you in, you have to promise not to make me just another speed bump on the Sebastian Hughes girlfriend superhighway."

He stared down at her. Her thick, dark hair hung in long waves past her shoulders. She had on a figure-hugging camisole, a pair of skintight jeans and no shoes. Her pretty little feet had delicately painted red nails. And she looked small and feminine. And he knew that he couldn't just move ahead the way he usually did with his damn-the-consequences attitude, no matter how much he wanted her.

Julia needed more from him. For once, he wanted to deliver. But he didn't know if he had anything to give. Could he keep a promise not to break her heart?

Did he want to?

Hell, yes, he did want to. He'd never felt for anyone what he felt for Julia. She was the last person in the world he'd want to hurt.

"Julia, give me a chance," he said, his voice husky with desire.

She stood back and held open the door. He stepped over the threshold and took in her house. Though she'd only been here for a few months, she'd taken the time to decorate. In the hallway sat a small framed photo of Julia in her cap and gown at college graduation, with two older people he guessed were her parents. He picked the frame up and looked at it as she closed the door behind him.

"You don't talk about your parents much," he said. "Would you like to invite them to visit?"

"I wish I could, but they died five years ago."

"Oh. Julia, I'm sorry."

"They died shortly after that photo was taken. I guess it was time for me to grow up," she said.

"But that doesn't mean you were ready to."

"No, I wasn't," she admitted. "Come into the living room. I'll get you a glass of wine."

She left him standing there. He looked down at the photo, feeling like an ass for having worked with her for two years without once asking about her family. What kind of person would do that?

He vowed to himself that he would start making up for lost time.

* * *

Julia opened the cabinet and found a second wine-glass. The last thing she wanted to do was be with Sebastian while she was in this kind of mood. She'd been feeling lonely and melancholy—and like she was in the wrong place in her life. And then he'd shown up.

He looked good—better than she wanted him to. She kept hoping that the lust she felt for him would simply fade away, but no. No chance. Every time she saw him, she felt a fierce desire for him that wasn't going away.

"You okay in there?" he called from the living room.

"Yes," she said. She pulled out the breakfast tray she used every morning and put the wine bottle, their glasses and some snacks on it. She didn't have a sophisticated palate, as she was sure Sebastian did. She just ate cheddar-flavored popcorn with her wine and some fresh fruit. It would have to do.

She hefted the tray and carried it out to the living room. Sebastian had taken off his suit jacket and tie, and he'd rolled up his shirtsleeves. His sock-clad feet were propped up on the glass coffee table, and there was an NBA game on the TV.

"Uh-uh. We're not watching sports tonight."

"I just wanted to catch the score," he said, getting to his feet and taking the tray from her. "I wouldn't dare get in between you and your DVR." He winked at her, and she felt heat rise to her face. He was sexy as hell—and he knew it.

She scooped up the remote, hit the button for the DVR selections and found the show she wanted to watch.

Though now that he was here, she doubted she'd be able to concentrate and enjoy it. Instead she'd probably just sit next to him wishing he'd unbutton his shirt buttons so she could see more of his chest.

She was pathetic. She'd turned into a sex-crazed woman because Sebastian had kissed her. One kiss, she thought. That was all it had taken to make her rethink everything she thought she knew about herself.

It was a spectacular kiss, though.

She handed him a wineglass and took one for herself. She almost apologized for not having the right cheese and crackers to go with the wine, but she stopped herself. If he wanted to be with a nice, regular girl from Texas, he would just have to get used to her ways. Right? Right.

"To new relationships," Sebastian said, toasting her.

"Cheers," she said, clinking her glass against his before taking a sip. She maintained eye contact while she sipped, as her father had taught her to do when she'd first gotten old enough to drink.

She noticed that Sebastian did it, too. But maybe he was just flirting with her. When he looked at her like that, she could understand why women fell for him... hell, she was doing it right now.

"I might not be the best company tonight."

"I'm not either. I just needed to see you," he said.

His words caught her off guard and touched her as nothing else could have, but she didn't want him to know that. "I'm glad."

"You're not giving an inch, are you?" he asked.

"What do you mean?"

"You can't let down your guard," he said.

"I'm afraid to. I'm worried that I'm just letting you take advantage of me."

"Julia, I don't think you're the kind of woman who lets anyone take advantage of you."

"It's tough with you, Sebastian. You're very… persuasive."

He gave her a half smile. "I'm used to having my way."

"Duh," she said.

He grabbed a handful of popcorn. "I like this."

"Sorry, I don't have cheese."

He looked confused for a second. "No, I mean *this*. Us."

She blushed. "Sorry," she said again.

He watched her for a second. "Julia, I'm sorry I never asked about your parents."

"My…? Oh. Well, why would you have?" she asked.

"You know everything about my family. You visit my father for me, and I never once wondered about your family."

She took a sip of her wine and grinned at him. "You're you-centric."

"I am, aren't I? That's my dad's fault."

"How is Christian to blame for that?" she asked.

"He told me I was the center of the universe. And I believed him."

That startled a laugh out of her. Sebastian could be alarmingly charming when he wanted to be.

"Is there any amount of money I can offer you to put the game back on?"

She shook her head. "It's time to be Julia-centric."

"Jules, baby—"

"Stop it. You're making me like a nickname that I hate."

"Why do you hate it?" he asked.

She took another sip of her wine. "In middle school, some kids used to call me Jules Verne. I liked to read sci-fi and I guess they thought it was funny."

"Julia, I never meant to make you feel bad. I was just teasing," he said.

"I know. Which is why I never made a big deal about it."

"Until I asked you to break up with Cici and you blew up at me."

"You had that one coming," she said. "You should have known better than to ask me to do that."

"I should have. But I'm glad I did because now I get the chance to know the real Julia Fitzgerald. And I wouldn't trade that for the world."

She could hardly believe her ears. There was something about Sebastian tonight that was very sincere and sweet—something she'd never seen before. The combination of his charm, sincerity and sexy good looks was deadly. Especially when he was saying things she'd always wanted to hear from a man.

She didn't stand a chance—and she knew it.

Five

Sebastian enjoyed being with Julia much more than he would have enjoyed being in the hustle and bustle of the polo club, which surprised him. Normally an evening on a woman's couch had him faking an emergency text from the office—something Julia would see right through. But the point was that he didn't want to leave.

He liked sitting next to her and listening to her rant about commercials that demeaned the intelligence of the average viewer. He liked her laugh, too. He rarely heard it in the office. The show they were watching had a lot of zingers between the male and female leads, and Julia laughed a full-bodied, sensual laugh at each one.

When they finished the episodes she'd recorded they'd almost finished a bottle of wine. Julia was looking very relaxed—and very sexy. She turned off the DVR and clicked another button to turn on some music.

"I can't stand silence," she said.

"Why not?" he asked as she stood to clean up the snacks.

"I had to live in my parents' house for six months after they died. I didn't have a job or money or anything, and the house was so quiet," she said. She glanced over at him. "Do you know what I mean? Was it like that after your mom died?"

"No. It wasn't the same for me. I still had my dad, so I was focused on keeping him healthy."

"You have a great dad," she said.

Sebastian knew that. He'd heard it his whole life. But to be honest, he'd taken his dad for granted until the cancer scare. He'd always just assumed that Christian Hughes would live forever because he was such a force to be reckoned with. Seeing him sick and almost losing him had shaken Sebastian to the core.

"I'm glad Dad is doing better now."

"Me, too. I'm glad I'm getting to know him. He's a charmer, like you," Julia said as she carried the tray into the kitchen.

"Like me?"

"Stop it. You know you can be charming when you put your mind to it."

He put his wineglass down and walked up behind Julia. He put one arm around her waist and drew her back against his chest, lowering his head so his chin rested on her shoulder.

"Can I?" he asked.

She turned her head, and her big eyes captivated him instantly. "I don't want to like you, but I can't help myself."

He hugged her tight. "Lucky for me," he said.

"I wanted to dance with you last night," she admitted.

"In the Star Room?"

"Yes."

"Why didn't you say something?" he asked.

She shrugged. "It didn't seem right."

"Let's dance now. No one can see us but the moon," he whispered in her ear, turning her around and taking her hand.

"Really?"

"Yes," he said. He led her into the living room and opened the doors to the large patio that overlooked the ocean. Sea grass and dunes protected their privacy. He found a music channel on the television that played love songs and then drew Julia into his arms.

He danced her around the living room, using all the knowledge he could remember from his seventh-grade group dance classes. "I'm afraid the best I can manage is a turning box step."

"I can't even do that. Maybe an electric slide."

"Not really a romance dance," he said.

"Are you romancing me?" she asked.

"I am," he said. He put his hands on her hips and they swayed together to Michael Bublé singing "Call Me Irresponsible." He found that ironic, wondering if he was being irresponsible right now. Was letting this relationship develop a mistake? He was making unspoken promises he wasn't sure he could keep, but walking away was no longer an option.

He wanted to share that bond he'd seen between Geoff and Amelia tonight. He now understood why Richard had been so devastated when his marriage ended. His friend had seen a glimpse of what life between a man and a woman could really be like, and then he'd had it snatched away.

Had Richard chosen the wrong woman, or were all relationships simply destined to end?

The next song was Percy Sledge singing "When a Man Loves a Woman." Julia closed her eyes and started moving her hips to the music, rubbing her body against his. The tips of her breasts brushed against his chest, and it took him only a second to realize she wasn't wearing a bra beneath her camisole. He put his hands on her hips and pulled her even closer.

Holding her this way made him believe this was where he was meant to be. It didn't matter that he wasn't thinking with his brain. It felt like everything in his life had narrowed down to this woman. He felt so lucky to be here with her.

She'd given him more than he'd expected, and he wanted everything she had to offer him—every last bit of Julia. He needed to claim her for his own, and nothing was going to stop him.

Except maybe Julia. But she wrapped her arms around his neck and stood up on her tiptoes to kiss him; he knew she wasn't going to send him home.

It was now or never. And he was choosing now.

Julia had never taken much time for personal relationships. Losing her parents had scared her, and she'd reacted by deciding to take care of her financial future first, always figuring that the rest of her life would sort itself out sometime. But it hadn't.

When she'd started working for Sebastian, she'd gotten even further away from finding a person to share her life with. But with Sebastian's arms around her, she felt like she was finally letting herself have…love? Could it be? Or was she confusing lust and love? If she was, she could be in serious danger.

She soon lost track of her thoughts as he slipped his hands under her camisole and slid them across her back. His hands were big and warm as he rubbed them up her spine and cupped her shoulder blades. His movements caused the fabric of her top to rub over her bare nipples, making them harden even more than the feel of Sebastian's arms around her had. She wanted more.

She really hadn't had that many lovers. Two guys in college, but that was it. Tony had taken her virginity in the back of his Mercedes-Benz. They'd had sex two more times before he had moved on to another girl, and then she'd dated a guy her senior year—Michael. They'd actually lived together. She'd thought...who knew what she'd thought.

She shifted, trying to get closer to him, but the fabric between them frustrated her. She reached for his shirt and drew it out of the waistband of his pants so she could tunnel her fingers underneath it and feel the warm skin of his back. She wanted to see his chest.

She fumbled with the buttons of his shirt. He unbuttoned it smoothly and quickly and took it off. His chest was smooth and nearly hairless, with just a small dusting between his nipples and a thin line that disappeared into his waistband. Before she knew what she was doing, she was tracing that line.

Circling his belly button, she saw his penis jump in reaction to her touch. She scraped her nail around the edge of his belly button, and his breath sawed in. She could tell he liked that.

She bent down and licked his stomach, using her teeth to tease him with little bites. His hands tightened in her hair, and she slowly nibbled her way down toward his belt. Then she worked her way back up until she was standing again. She brought her hand up between his legs and stroked his erection through his pants.

She reached lower and cupped him, and he let out a groan. He reached between them and undid his pants, and she slid her hand inside to find his hot, hard length. He found the hem of her shirt and drew it up her body until her breasts were revealed to his gaze.

"You are very pretty, Julia," he said.

She flushed as he stared at her breasts. He touched her softly, using only the tips of his fingers on the full globes of her breasts, and then rubbed his thumb back and forth over her nipple until she was almost crazy from his touch.

She felt a pulse between her legs—and wetness. She wanted him. She needed him right now. She reached for the button on her jeans and unfastened it, desperate to feel his hand between her legs.

He stopped her. "Let me do that," he growled.

The feel of his hands reaching between their bodies and unzipping her pants nearly undid her. She felt his fingers dip beneath the fabric of her bikini panties, and then his finger brushed her. She shivered and went up on her tiptoes as she continued to stroke his erection.

He lowered his head to hers and kissed her as he had last night. Desire was raging through her. She rubbed the tips of her nipples against his chest and moaned. He plunged his hand into her hair and held her as he plundered her mouth. His other hand reached lower until he could slip the tip of his finger inside her body.

She shuddered as she felt his finger start to enter her. It had been a long time since a man had touched her, and she knew she was going to come. But she didn't want to—not yet. She wanted him right there with her when she went over the edge.

She tried to bring him along, but he took her hand from his erection and held it loosely. "I want you to come for me."

"I don't think I could stop if I tried," she said breathlessly.

He pushed his finger farther into her, and his thumb found the center of her passion again. Rubbing lightly up and down, he brought her so close to the edge she could hardly stand it.

He lowered his head and took the tip of her breast in his mouth, suckling her deep and hard. The next thing she knew, stars exploded between her legs as every nerve ending in her body started to pulse. The explosion rocked her and sent waves radiating out from where he touched her.

She couldn't stop rubbing against his hand, and the sensations continued to build. He switched his attention to her other breast as he took his hand from between her legs, leaving her weak in the knees.

He lifted her into his arms and carried her to the couch, where he laid her down and gazed at her for a moment.

"Take your pants off, Julia."

She pushed her tight jeans down her legs as he watched. Sebastian kneeled beside her and reached out to touch her hip, drawing his fingers down her thigh toward her knee and then back up again to the junction between her legs. He skimmed her neatly trimmed hair and brought his fingers to his face. "I love the smell of you."

No man had ever loved anything about her. Not the way Sebastian did. She wanted to be his completely.

"Are you… I'm not on the pill," she said.

"I don't have a condom," he said.

She bit her lower lip. "I bought a box this afternoon."

"You did?"

"Yes. I… You… Let's just say I was hopeful that we'd be able to use them sometime soon."

"That seems…"

"Not me, I know. But once I agreed to be with you, I wanted to be prepared. I don't want to look back and say you seduced me into this."

He kissed her deeply. "Me either. Where are they?" he asked.

"In the bathroom."

Now that they were talking and he wasn't touching her, she was starting to feel very exposed. But he stood up and pulled her up with him. "Show me your bedroom. And then let me make love to you all night long."

Sebastian was glad they had to slow down and come into her bedroom. As desperate as he was to get inside her beautiful body, he wanted their lovemaking to be perfect.

"Get undressed and get in bed. I'll be right back," he said.

He went into her bathroom and saw the box of condoms on the counter. Julia had invested herself in him and he was touched. He took off his pants and his socks. And then he took the box and went back into the bedroom. She'd turned off all the lights except for a small nightstand lamp that cast the room in a soft glow.

She lay in the center of the bed under the sheets, the pillows piled high behind her head and her thick hair fanning out around her. She was so sexy and captivating; he paused at the end of the bed just to look at her.

"Will you move the covers aside so I can see all of you?"

She hesitated. He knew he was asking for a lot. Despite being bold and brassy in the office, Julia was shy about her body. She slowly pushed the sheet down her body. Each curve that was revealed made him harder.

Her breasts were full, with large pinkish-brown nipples, which were hard. He remembered the velvet smoothness of them in his mouth. Her waist was small, and there was a slight curve to her belly. His eyes traveled to the dark hair that guarded her secrets and down long, toned legs, which were pressed close together as if she were afraid to reveal too much. He took the covers and flipped them back toward the foot of the bed. Then he took her ankles in his hands and drew her legs apart. She turned a bright red as he stared at her most feminine part.

He knelt on the bed and crawled up toward her, pausing to drop a kiss on her secrets and letting his tongue tease the bud that was the center of her pleasure. Then he moved up over her body.

He braced himself on his elbows and lowered his hips until he rested in the cradle of her thighs, shifting until he felt the humid warmth of her against him.

Then he pulled back, cursing. "I forgot the condom."

She laughed, and he reached for the box that he held crushed in one hand. He opened it and pulled out the packet.

He put it on as quickly as he could and then moved back over her. The wall of his chest brushed over those hard nipples of hers, and he rotated his shoulders so his chest hair abraded them.

Then he let his hips fall against hers. He moved his

hips until his tip was at the entrance of her body. He leaned in to her and bent his head so he could whisper directly into her ear.

"You are so sexy."

"You make me feel that way," she said.

"I want you."

"Me, too, Sebastian."

She tried to lift her hips and force him to take her, but he made her wait until she was moving frantically against him. Then he slipped inside her just slightly, so that she could feel him but still not have him as deep as she wanted.

She moaned and begged him for more, which got him harder than he'd ever been in his life. And slowly he gave her what she wanted. He kept her with him the entire time, wanting her to come when he did. He soon felt the telltale tightening at the base of his spine and was surprised by how quickly he was going to come.

But this was Julia, and nothing was normal with her. All of his reactions were off the scale with this woman. He clasped her hands and stretched her right arm over her head as he slid all the way home, making her gasp. He plunged deep into her body, and his hips pistoned in and out until he heard a roaring in his ears. He felt the tightening of her body around his and then he could hold it no longer—he exploded.

He called her name and thrust into her three more times as his body emptied itself of everything. Then he collapsed against her breasts.

She wrapped her arms around his shoulders and held him to her. Her fingers toyed with the hair at the nape of his neck as her breathing slowed. He knew he couldn't fall asleep on top of her, but he wanted to sleep right there in her arms, wanted to let the solace he felt continue to wrap around him.

He pushed himself up on his elbows and looked down at her. She smiled up at him.

"I want to spend the night," he said. "Can I?"

She nodded. "I want you to, as well."

He moved the pillows around until he was comfortable and then pulled her into his arms.

She shifted, her breasts brushing against the side of his body and her hand drifting low on his stomach to rest against his hip bone. He held her close and knew that even though only the moon had witnessed their becoming lovers, the world was going to know about it soon. Julia had changed something inside of him that he'd never realized could be changed—and nothing would ever be the same.

Six

Julia spent her days working like crazy—and her nights in Sebastian's arms. The month of June was flying by, and she still hadn't figured out exactly what the future held for her, but for the first time since her parents' death it didn't matter. She wasn't planning carefully for her next step. Instead she was simply living her life in the warm embrace of the sexy man who was stealing her heart.

She made sure that every detail of the season's polo matches went off without a hitch. She visited Christian, whose health improved a little more each day. She suspected his days in rehab were almost over and had no problem imagining him sitting next to Sebastian in the owner's box by the end of the season.

Tonight was a low-key weeknight, and there were no big events. She hadn't seen Sebastian all day, but he had left her a message telling her to meet him on the beach behind her house. Her skin tingled at the very thought of it.

She went home, changed into a sundress and made it down to the beach just as the sun was beginning to set. Sebastian was nowhere to be seen, but two Adirondack chairs sat side by side facing the ocean. In front of them was a fire pit with some low coals burning.

There was a note tacked to the cooler that informed her he would be right back.

She sat down in one of the chairs and closed her eyes, enjoying the summer breeze and the evening. She wanted nothing more than to figure out how to make this relationship last. And it *was* a relationship—not an affair.

They spent most nights in her bed, and they ate breakfast together almost every day. When they were at the office, he sometimes pulled her into his arms behind closed doors simply because he had to kiss her—his words.

She had no idea where this was going, and despite his reassurances that he was crazy about her, she was nervous. She needed a plan. She needed to know what the next step was going to be so she could believe that she wasn't going to end up with a broken heart.

Sebastian had arranged an interview for her with the VP of PR for Clearwater, John Martin.

The interview was promising, and she was flattered that Sebastian's recommendation had led to it. She was excited about it, mainly because she knew the moment she took that job she'd be saying goodbye to Sebastian, the boss. And then she could focus on Sebastian, the man.

"Hello, Julia."

She stood up at the sound of his voice and saw that

he was loaded down with a picnic basket. He wore a pair of faded, low-slung jeans and a lightweight summer sweater. His feet were bare.

"What can I do to help?"

"You can sit back and talk to me. I've got dinner under control."

She sat back down.

"Do you want a drink?"

"Yes, please," she said.

He opened the cooler, took out a chilled wineglass and poured her some pinot grigio. He handed her a glass and then poured one for himself. She held hers up to his and said, "To dinners on the beach."

He clinked her glass and then went back to the cooler. "What happened at the office after I left?"

"Not much. That Broadway producer canceled his event for next week. I did a little scrambling but found another sponsor for it."

"Good."

"I e-mailed you the details."

He nodded. "Did John get back to you with a job offer? I know June is the end of our agreement. We'll be right in the thick of polo here."

She took a sip of her wine. "Yes, he did."

"Are you going to take it?"

She didn't know yet, but she knew she couldn't say that to Sebastian. He'd done his part, getting her an interview for a job where she could run the show and advance her career. But now she wasn't sure she wanted it.

"I haven't decided yet. But either way, you're off the hook."

"No, I'm not," he said, handing her a plate with grilled salmon, sautéed new potatoes and steamed asparagus.

He made his own plate and sat down next to her.

She was impressed he went to all this trouble for her. She picked at the food, not ready to have this conversation with him. She wanted Sebastian to be the self-involved boss she'd always known him to be instead of the kind, caring man she'd come to know. It would make accepting the job so much easier. It would make leaving him so much simpler.

In the past few weeks, she'd started to fall for him. Okay, she'd fallen for him completely—and that was probably the dumbest thing she'd ever done. She wasn't the kind of person who fell in love easily, she thought, but somehow, with Sebastian, she had.

"If that job isn't what you had in mind, don't take it. There's no hurry for you to leave. I have other colleagues I can get you an interview with," he said.

That made her care even more for him. He wasn't just using money to ease his way out of his obligation. He was making sure she had everything she needed to be happy, and that meant more to her than she could say.

"Sebastian, you've done your best by me, and I can't ask for anything more."

He looked at her with a smile that took her breath away. "I wish you would," he said.

Sebastian loved the way Julia looked tonight. She was simply dressed, but she looked amazing sitting on the beach by the small fire. Sharing the end of the day with her was something he'd gotten used to, and he didn't want to give it up.

He was coming to depend on her personally as well as professionally, and that should have worried him, but it didn't. There wasn't a relationship in his life he didn't know how to control and keep on track, and he couldn't see why this one would be any different.

He noticed that she was shivering, and he pulled a cashmere shawl out of the picnic basket that he'd purchased for her earlier in the day.

"Lean forward," he said.

She did, and he draped it over her shoulders.

"This is really nice," she said.

"I'm glad you like it. It's for you."

"You picked this out for me? Without any help?"

"I have my ways, and I can't reveal them," he said.

She laughed. "Who did you scheme with?"

"My *dad*. He told me that I worked you too hard and that you needed a nice night of relaxing and a present. And he wanted me to thank you for your brilliant inspiration that allows him to see what's going on at the Seven Oaks."

Thanks to Julia, Sebastian had put in a direct satellite link to the polo matches that beamed a private broadcast to Christian's room. His father hadn't missed a match all season. Julia was one of the most thoughtful people Sebastian had ever met.

"Can you believe how well Nicolas played today? I think he really is the best player of our time," she said.

"I agree. He is a dynamo on the field," Sebastian said. And off it, as well. The man never stopped moving. He was very popular in the VIP tents and more and more women were trickling in as the days progressed. Every one of them wanted a piece of the star player. "I'm concerned about Vanessa. She was asking about him the other night, and Nicolas already broke her heart once."

"Your sister is a smart woman. She won't let him hurt her again."

"You think so?" Sebastian asked her.

"Yes," she said, but she wasn't sure. She was falling for Sebastian and she knew that it wasn't smart, yet here she was having this romantic picnic with him.

She finished her meal and he tucked the plates back into the basket. He stoked the fire and drew their chairs closer together.

"Why did you invite me here tonight?" she asked.

"To say thank you."

"But I haven't done anything this week that I wouldn't have done before, and you never even bought me dinner," she said.

He loved that she didn't let him get away with anything. Many of the women he'd dated just let him have his way—but not Julia.

"I totally took you for granted before, and I'm trying to make it up to you. You are coming to mean more to me, Julia, than I ever expected."

She tipped her head to the side and stared at him in the flickering glow of the fire's light. "You, too."

"Me, too?"

"I didn't want to fall for you, Sebastian. I've seen how long most of your relationships last. But this time it feels different. I guess that's because I think I'm different."

"You are," he said. She cared about the people around her, and because of that, he was slowly coming to see the world through her eyes. His priorities were changing. For the first time, he was living his life and not worrying about moving ahead and conquering the next big thing.

"I'm glad you feel that way. I think that's part of the reason I'm reluctant to take John's offer."

"Why?"

"I was thinking that I could stay in your office but take on more of a managerial role instead of being your girl Friday. We make a really good team."

"We do," he said. But he didn't know if working together would be a good idea now that they were sleeping together. He was distracted by her. He wanted to pull her into his arms and make love to her at the oddest moments during the day, and that wouldn't be very appropriate in their office back in Manhattan.

He had given her his word about the job, doing his best to find her a good one. But seeing her every day had become important to him, and he knew he didn't want to let her slip away now.

He couldn't.

Damn. When had she slipped past his guard?

"Sebastian?"

"Huh?"

"What do you think about that?" she asked.

She wanted to talk about it, but he didn't have the words. He could smooth talk anyone into anything, but not Julia. She was different. Being with her had changed his life.

And that scared him.

Sebastian Hughes, who'd never let anything frighten him, was suddenly afraid of losing this woman.

"Let's go for a walk. I want to show you something." He stood up and offered her his hand, but she just stared at it.

"I guess that's an answer."

She rose and started to walk away, but he stopped her.

"I don't have an answer for you. I'm not sure how to put my emotions into words. I only know that you are important to me, and I'm not sure working together will be what either of us needs."

"Will you consider it?"

He nodded. "I don't want to lose you."

She turned and put her arms around his waist, hugging him close. "I feel the same way. I'm falling for you, Sebastian."

He had no response. He only knew that having her in his arms made him feel like everything was right in his world. But try as he might, he couldn't tell her that.

Julia dressed for work the next morning with care. She had a jam-packed day with lots of VIPs to attend to. Sebastian had been gone when she woke up, but there had been a note on her table saying he wanted to see her for dinner that night.

She thought last night had changed the dynamic in their relationship, and she felt like they might have a chance of making it last for more than the summer. But she had to wait for Sebastian to tell her what he thought.

As she drove to work, she saw the polo ponies being exercised and realized how much she loved this place and the life she had here. She didn't want to risk losing any part of it. In fact, she wanted to build on it.

And the nights in Sebastian's arms were part of that. It was only once she knew that she was leaving this that she'd realized how much she wanted to stay.

She would miss talking to Christian every day and hearing his stories about starting the polo club. She'd miss talking to celebrities and their handlers and making sure that all details of their visits were taken care of.

She stopped and looked around her, realizing if Sebastian didn't agree to her idea she was going to have to leave. She didn't think she could stand to keep working at Clearwater and not work closely with Sebastian, especially if their affair ended. She'd miss him too much.

She knew more about the inner workings of the celebrity media machine than most people did—and she liked it.

She entered her office, gathered the faxes and went over the itineraries and menus for the day's events.

Grant Vineyards and Wines was sponsoring a pre-polo match event and of course the sheikh would be attending. Despite his new bride, women were still flocking to see him and hoping to catch his eye. Julia didn't envy the sheikh's young bride. She knew she'd be extremely jealous.

Though rumor had it that the sheikh was very much in love with his new wife, and that made Julia a bit envious. She wanted Sebastian to be in love with her.

Wait a minute, she thought. Was that really what she wanted?

She sat down in her office chair. Of course it was. She had fallen in love with her boss…soon to be ex-boss. She didn't have to think hard to figure out why.

Once he'd known she was leaving, he'd relaxed his guard and their working relationship had changed. He'd changed. And so had she.

She bit her lower lip. Things had only changed once he realized she was leaving. Was that some kind of omen?

The phone rang. It was him. She reached for it but stopped before she answered. She needed a minute to figure this out.

She didn't want to end up like all of Sebastian's other women, sitting alone at a table with a box from Tiffany's.

She imagined her cell phone ringing with a call from his assistant.

She'd seen how he'd walked away when things got too intense for him. Why did she think she'd be any different? Had she scared him with her request to step things up professionally?

She was a simple girl from Texas, not a sophisticated woman used to wheeling and dealing—and handling a man like Sebastian.

She was scared—really scared that she might have finally let Sebastian get the better of her. And that was the one thing she'd promised herself she'd never let happen. But it had happened, and now she was between a rock and a hard place.

The phone rang again. She answered it.

"This is Julia."

"You okay? I called just a minute ago and got voice mail," he said.

"I'm fine. Sorry about that. What's up?"

"I need you to go down to the stables and see if you can find Richard. He's been spending a lot of time there. I need to talk to him right away about the Henderson deal."

"I'm on it."

"Great. I'll be in the office in an hour. I'm visiting Dad, and then I have to stop by the heliport and pick up the senator. Is that right?"

"Yes. I'll text you the details. Should Richard call your cell?"

"Definitely."

"I'll take care of it," she said.

"Thank you, Julia. And don't forget about our dinner tonight. We need to talk."

"I haven't forgotten," she said, a sick feeling in the pit

of her stomach. He hung up and she sat there, staring at her desk. Their conversation was like a million they'd had before—all business and to the point, until the end. Something was up. What did he need to tell her?

She shook her head. She was turning into some kind of desperate woman, and she hated it. Whatever he had to say, she would be fine.

She put her phones to voice mail and went outside the polo club office and got on her golf cart. Getting around Seven Oaks was easier with the aid of a golf cart. She drove through the early morning mist toward the stables in search of Richard.

Though Sebastian had mentioned not being able to get through to Richard's cell, Julia tried anyway and left him a message. She pulled up outside the stables but when she went inside she didn't find anyone but a couple of grooms.

One of the sheikh's ponies poked his head over the stable door. She walked close to the glossy black horse, knowing that no one but the sheikh and his trainer ever rode the horse.

She stood there, seeing the power in those black eyes. Power didn't necessarily come from money. Sebastian would have it no matter how much he had in the bank. She wanted to reach out but stopped when she heard the sound of hooves behind her.

She turned around to find Catherine returning from working out a horse.

"Hi, Julia. What's up?" Catherine asked.

"I'm looking for Richard. Have you seen him this morning?"

She quickly shook her head. "Why?"

"I thought he spent a lot of time down here. If he does show up will you ask him to call Sebastian?"

"Sure," said Catherine, dismounting and walking the horse away.

Julia left the stables feeling more distracted than ever. Today should be one of the happiest days of her life—she'd just realized she was in love. Instead, those emotions just made her realize that she was more vulnerable than ever.

She didn't want to lose everything she'd worked for, but losing Sebastian would be worse. She didn't realize love could feel this intense. She needed Sebastian Hughes, and he wasn't known for being there for her.

Seven

Sebastian had avoided his office all day. Last night on the beach, he'd felt fear for the first time, and he knew that meant one thing. He couldn't keep seeing Julia.

She was becoming his Achilles' heel. And he'd always been careful to make sure he had no weaknesses. The thought of building a life with her personally and professionally was too much for him. It felt too dangerous.

So he'd spoken to the chef about arranging an intimate meal at the house and ordered a nice piece of jewelry from Tiffany's. He felt like a bastard as he made his plans for the evening, but he knew that the only way they were both going to survive was if he did this.

He had no idea how to be in a long-term relationship. And if he didn't promote her, Julia was leaving him anyway. She had to. How could she stay with a man who didn't respect her enough to see just how valuable her skills were?

He shook his head. It was pride that was motivating him. But when hadn't it been? He understood pride, which was why he had done a good job of running the polo club and keeping his own business going at the same time.

He needed someone to talk to, but Richard was dealing with his own crap and Geoff was back in London. He was on his own. And he could only handle this the best way he knew how.

He walked into the dining room to await a chat with the chef.

The last few weeks had been more than he'd ever expected to have with any woman. He loved the hot nights making love in her bed, but he also enjoyed the quiet moments watching TV with her, or glancing over at her during a polo match and seeing her smile at him.

If he were a different man maybe he'd be able to figure out how to make this work, figure out a way to make her stay with him. But he wasn't a different man.

He heard the door open behind him and turned around to see Marc there. "I wanted to double-check the timing for your dinner, sir."

"Drinks and appetizers when Julia arrives, and then I'll signal the waiter when we're ready for dinner."

Marc nodded and left.

Sebastian walked nervously around the room, staring at the box. It was the same gift he gave every woman he broke up with, and he didn't know if he could do it. He didn't know if he was going to be able to treat Julia like every other woman in his life, though he tried to convince himself he could.

He walked around the walnut-paneled room and stopped under the portrait of his father. The painting had been done by a prominent American portrait artist and portrayed his father in the year he'd founded the club. The same year that Christian had met Lynette and started courting her.

His father had a full head of hair and looked down at Sebastian with that young face. It was hard to picture his dad as a young man because most of his life, well, Christian had simply seemed older and wiser.

He'd married Lynette because of her family connections, and that marriage had been a cold one. Sebastian and Vanessa had lived that firsthand.

He didn't want to repeat the mistakes his father had made. He didn't want to spend his life in a cold marriage—or in no marriage at all. And he didn't want to let the right woman slip through his fingers now.

Was he being too hasty by ending things with Julia tonight?

He heard the door open behind him. The waiter came in to place the wine bucket and a tray of crudités on the table. Sebastian's nerves were frayed.

Julia was just a woman, he thought. She was like every other woman he'd ever dated. Tonight he would end things with her once and for all. He might find another woman in his life to marry or he might not. But he knew that he couldn't be with Julia. He couldn't be with her until he figured out a way to manage the emotions she brought so easily to the surface in him.

The door opened again, and he turned around.

She was here.

Julia wore a lovely gray cocktail dress that enhanced her smooth white skin. Her long hair was down, and her lips were glossy and luscious. For a minute, he couldn't breathe as he stared at her.

He took a step forward, and then two, and then he had her in his arms. He tunneled his fingers through her hair as he kissed her, crushing her to him.

The thought of not being able to do this made his hands shake. He pulled back and looked down at her. She stared up at him.

"Are you okay?" she asked.

He nodded. "I am now."

He held her in his arms, knowing that he couldn't end things with her. He couldn't let her walk away from him, whatever it was that she made him feel. He was afraid to admit it might be love.

"Come sit down. I have a lot to say to you tonight," he said.

He led the way to the table. Julia stopped dead in her tracks as she got close enough to see the Tiffany's box placed on her plate.

"Really, Sebastian? You can't be serious."

Julia could only shake her head. She was furious—and devastated. But anger was the thing she wanted to hold on to. He'd just kissed her like she was the missing half of his soul and then she'd turned around and seen this.

"I can't believe you."

"It's not what you are thinking. Please sit down so we can talk."

"Talk? I don't want to talk. I thought you'd changed, Sebastian. But this…well, this shows me you are still the man who wanted his assistant to break up with his girlfriend."

"This has nothing to do with Cici," he said. He

walked back to her. "You don't know anything about what I'm feeling right now."

"You're right, I don't," she said, feeling the first sting of tears at the back of her eyes. "I thought…I thought I had been getting to know the real man these last few weeks."

"You have been," he assured her. He put his hand out as if to touch her arm, and she backed away.

"Please don't touch me."

"It's not what you think," he said.

For a minute she started to listen, but she knew what that box meant. "Stop. I'm not content to take scraps of caring you throw my way. And I think I deserve better than that."

Sebastian rubbed the back of his neck. "I want better than that for you, too."

She thought he cared about her. Was he doing this because she wanted to work with him as his equal? "I don't get this. Are you afraid that I'll get too close? That you won't be able to keep me at arm's length if we work together?"

"You thought we'd just keep on this way?" he asked her.

"Yes, I did. I'm starting to care for you. Hell, why hedge my bets? I want to stay here. I don't want to leave you, Sebastian."

"I don't think we can work together anymore."

Those words just confirmed what she already knew. He needed her to go quietly out of his life. She wasn't going to take a job working for John Martin. Maybe she'd just go back to Texas where she could resume a quiet life far away from the glitz and glitter of the Bridgehampton Polo Club.

But before she left she wanted him to understand that. "I guess we can't," she said.

"Julia, it's not that I don't want you in the office with me, but I can't look at you the same way. You are a distraction. Once I see you in the office, all I want to do is pull you into my arms. And that's not what either of us wants."

Speak for yourself, she thought. She wanted to feel his arms around her whenever she laid eyes on him. She'd liked working with him publicly and then seeing him at night when it was only the two of them.

Sharing every second of the day together was exactly what she wanted, but that wasn't going to happen. "I think you are scared."

"I am," he admitted. "No woman has ever affected me the way you do, and I don't want to make a mistake that I will regret the rest of my life. You asked me once about my mother, and I hedged because I didn't want to tell you that my father married Lynette because she was beautiful and then he found himself stuck in a loveless marriage. She married him for his money."

"I'm sorry your father made the choice to stay with someone he didn't love. But you don't have to repeat his mistakes," she said.

"I know. I'm just trying to figure it out. I made a promise to myself that I'd stay unencumbered and free. I don't want to be trapped, or trap anyone. Until I met you, that worked for me, Julia."

"And now?"

"I don't know. I told you that I'm scared, and that is the truth. I don't know if I should keep you by my side or send you away. I brought you here tonight to end things, but the longer I waited for you, the harder it was for me to believe that I could really say goodbye."

She stared at him, afraid to believe what she was hearing. But she knew he wouldn't lie to her. Sebastian didn't lie to anyone. He was a straight shooter.

"What are you trying to say?"

He took her hand in his. "I love you, Julia Fitzgerald."

She started to speak, to confess her love for him, but he put his finger over her lips. "Let me finish. Loving you is the scariest thing I've ever experienced, and I don't know which way to turn or what decision to make."

"I think we should be making decisions together," she said.

"Why?"

"Because I love you, too, Sebastian. I have been trying to figure out how to say those words to you. I've been trying to figure out how to make you see that I don't want to live without you."

Sebastian pulled her into his arms and held her close. He whispered his love to her again, and she held him tightly to her. She was afraid to believe what he'd told her, afraid that this might all be a dream. But the next morning, when she woke up in his arms, she was able to start believing that it might be true.

And then after the trip to Bridgehampton Jewelers for an engagement ring, she knew it was starting to feel real not just to her but to Sebastian, as well.

"Let's go tell my dad."

"Really?" she asked. "Once you do, he'll tell the world."

"I'm ready for the world to know," Sebastian said. He pulled her into his arms and kissed her deeply.

Christian was watching the video monitor of the horses when they walked into his room. Sebastian had his arm around her and Julia knew she had the biggest smile of her life on her face.

Christian arched one eyebrow at them. "I see that Sebastian has made you a happy woman."

"He has," Julia said.

"I'll make her even happier once she becomes my wife. We're getting married, Dad."

"About damned time," Christian said.

* * * * *

MAGNATE'S MISTRESS-FOR-A-MONTH

YVONNE LINDSAY

With special acknowledgment to the lovely,
generous and knowledgeable Genevie Hogg.
Thanks so much for your time and for opening up
the fascinating world of polo to me.

One

Sebastian was right. He seriously needed to get laid.

Richard Wells rolled off his stomach—and off the early morning discomfort that painfully reminded him of his newly permanent single state. Funny how that hadn't been an issue in the whole year it had taken for his divorce to be finalized. Now his heart and mind were free, the rest of his body had decided to rapidly follow suit.

Birdsong penetrated his sleep-fogged mind—the sound was a welcome difference from the low hum of traffic and muted sirens he usually heard through his double-glazed high-rise windows—reminding him of his current location and the fact that this was his first vacation in far too long.

He lay there for a moment, relishing the sensation of the Seven Oaks Farm guesthouse's fine Egyptian cotton sheets against his bare skin. Yeah, he liked this feeling.

Freedom. It was a feeling he hadn't enjoyed in far too long.

Richard kicked away his covers. Vacation or not, he didn't want to stay in bed a moment longer. Always an early riser—in more ways than one, he smiled ruefully as he adjusted himself on his way to the bathroom—it would be sacrilege to waste even one second of the beautiful June morning that had begun to shine through the gauzy curtains on the window. Seb had been at him for months now to take some time out for R & R. The lure of polo, ponies and a plethora of beautiful people looking for a good time, not a long time, was just the medicine he needed.

Divorcing Daniella had taken more out of him than he'd wanted to admit—fiscally and personally. It still rankled that he'd allowed himself to be swayed by a beautiful face and an even more beautiful body. How could he not have seen past her facade to the avaricious creature beneath? Still, he'd finally broken free of her, and now it was time for new beginnings. New beginnings of a more casual nature. There was no way he was ready to embark on anything more permanent again.

Richard padded into the bathroom and turned on the shower, letting the cool stream of water refresh his body and his mind. He'd left the office so late last night he'd almost decided not to drive out to Seven Oaks. But the second he'd hit the Montauk Highway, he knew he'd done the right thing in giving in to the lure of fresh air and a peace he never quite managed to attain in the city.

He stepped out of the shower and grabbed a luxuriously thick, fluffy towel to dry off. Now that he was finally here, he was eager to get down to the stables and check out the ponies. It had been far too long since he'd allowed himself the downtime to indulge in the things he loved, riding being one of them. Seb had told him yesterday that Sheikh Adham Aal Ferjani's string of ponies for the polo season were exceptional. Now was probably a good time to find that out for himself. He dragged on a pair of jeans and a well-washed designer T-shirt before sliding his feet into a pair of butter-soft leather loafers.

The sun was an encroaching halo of light on the horizon as Richard let himself out of the guesthouse. He'd been too tired last night, and it had been too late for him to really appreciate his surroundings but now, in the dawn air, he could fully admire the beauty around him. He felt a sense of energy and promise that had been lacking from his world for too long.

Seven Oaks boasted several buildings, including a small apartment house for the grooms who cared for the horses as well as three barns and world-class polo fields. With the huge amount of sponsorship and money being thrown around in the coming months, the farm was most definitely the central pulse for what promised to be a high-stakes season. The Clearwater Media Cup, sponsored by the company he and Seb ran together, would start this coming weekend.

Several horses lifted their heads in interest as he passed their paddocks, one whickering softly. Richard felt his lips relax into a smile at the sound. Yeah, it had been far too long since he'd put aside the rigors of work and simply enjoyed life.

He leaned his arms across the top rail of the fence, hitched one foot on the lower rail and took a moment to watch the horses. Bit by bit the tension accumulated over the past few months—work pressure with the demands of his drawn-out divorce proceedings—started to drain from his shoulders.

Seb had been right about the ponies, if the handful in this field were anything to go by. Richard let his eyes roam over their forms, taking pleasure in the perfection of their powerful bodies and the graceful bow of their strong necks. Thoroughbred bloodlines showed clearly in each and every one.

The rhythmic thud of hooves on the hard-packed ground echoed a short distance away. Curious, Richard followed the noise.

Silhouetted by the rising sun, horse and rider appeared in one majestic silhouette as they cantered around another paddock. Despite the animal's obvious spirited nature, the rider left the reins loosely knotted on the pony's neck. The pony could stop and turn on a dime, guided by little more than the rider's thighs and subtle shifts of his supple, lightly muscled body as he gracefully wielded a polo stick, striking a white ball up and down the paddock.

Her body, Richard realized as the rider moved side on, revealing very feminine curves and the flick of a long, braided mass of hair down her back. Every nerve in his body knotted as he watched her, his eyes eagerly roaming the lean length of her legs clad in snug-fitting riding breeches, the way her gently rounded backside skimmed the saddle, her perfectly aligned spine and the straight set of her shoulders.

It was as if she and the horse had been carved from the same malleable substance, moving as one incredibly graceful, cohesive unit.

She appeared impervious to the slight chill in the early morning air. Impervious, too, to the man watching her. Richard found himself mesmerized and acknowledged the unbidden fire of need that began smoldering deep down, low in his groin. He wondered if she was one of Seb's staff and racked his memory for any mention of a particularly attractive groom or polo player, but he came up blank.

While the farm and the polo club had traditionally been Seb's father's domain, Seb had become very hands-on in the past couple of years as Christian Hughes waged war on the cancer that attacked him. No, if Seb had hired someone who looked like this, Richard would have heard about it, even if only in passing. Which only left the sheikh's team and staff, who were staying at the farm for the duration of the season.

Richard rubbed his chin reflectively. That could prove more difficult, depending on exactly what her role was in the sheikh's employ—if she even was on his payroll. The soft murmur of the rider's voice as she picked up the reins and encouraged the animal in the direction of the nearest barn galvanized Richard into action.

How hard could it be to find out who she was—and just how well he'd be able to get to know her? After all, it wasn't as if he was looking for forever.

Catherine Lawson slid from the saddle and handed the polo stick she'd been training the pony to become used to, to one of the junior grooms. The pony was a recent addition to her boss's string, and she'd been eager to try her out.

"How'd Ambrosia go?" the freckle-faced teen asked.

"Pretty good, but it'll be a while before she's up to the standards of those guys." Catherine nodded in the direction of the ponies that had been turned out into the fields last night after the afternoon practice.

"You want me to take care of her for you?"

"No, it's okay. I'll do it." Catherine smiled at the girl's eagerness.

Had she ever been that young and eager to work with the horses? She supposed she had, but it seemed like a long, long time ago. While she loved her work—loved horses above all else—she still held on to her dream of setting up her own riding stables one day. And, she reminded herself, if she slacked off in her current role, that day would be a great deal further away than it already was.

Catherine lifted off the saddle and stacked it on its peg before untacking the pony and sliding on a halter in place of the bridle. The pony butted her shoulder gently as she did so, raising a smile on Catherine's lips.

"Impatient, are we?" she crooned softly, rubbing her hand gently across Ambrosia's soft nose.

"You looked amazing out there. Are you a player?"

Catherine wheeled around to find the source of the deep male voice that stroked through the air. Ambrosia startled, jerking her head and Catherine's hand up high. Catherine took a minute to settle the pony, then felt her heart rate accelerate as she studied the man opposite.

A slow, languorous heat suffused her body. She knew this guy—she had seen his pictures in the business pages of the *Times* as well as featured in the glossy tabloids she was hopelessly addicted to. Richard Wells—business developer extraordinaire, business partner to Sebastian Hughes in Clearwater Media and totally out of her league.

Taller than her own five feet nine inches, she found herself having to look slightly up to meet clear gray eyes edged with sooty dark lashes. His nose was a straight blade of male perfection bisecting a face that photographed well but was even more handsome in person. Rich sable-brown hair was expertly cut but had been tousled by the morning breeze, leaving his forehead bare, and a smudge of whiskers shadowed his jaw.

She quelled the urgent burn of longing that simmered deep inside her. Last she'd heard, he was in the middle of a very messy divorce. If he was making a play for her now, which she fully suspected was the case given the light of interest burning in those beautiful eyes, then he wasn't her type at all. She wasn't prepared to potentially put herself in the limelight that was his world.

No doubt he'd lose interest soon enough when she made it clear she wasn't that kind of girl.

"No, I'm head groom to Sheikh Adham ben Khaleel ben Haamed Aal Ferjani," she replied, using her boss's name to full effect.

Usually, it had just the outcome she wanted. Most people, impressed or intimidated, would withdraw. Unfortunately, it looked as if Richard Wells wasn't "most people."

"Head groom, huh? You must be good for the sheikh to have a woman in that role."

She fought back the urge to bristle. His was a natural reaction and one she'd come across often in the twelve years she'd been in Sheikh Adham Aal Ferjani's employ. But there was a subtle double entendre in his words that rankled. The same entendre she'd sensed in his initial overture to her with his use of the word *player*.

"I earned my position with him, as does everyone in his employ. Now, if you'll excuse me, I have work to do."

"You have an accent. Where are you from?"

Catherine drew in a short breath. Didn't he get it? She

wasn't interested. Ambrosia shifted nervously, picking up on her tension. She laid a soothing hand on the mare's neck and murmured gently to her before answering.

"New Zealand. Although I haven't been back for a long time."

"A pity. It's a beautiful country."

"You can find beauty wherever you are. If you want to, that is."

"Good point," Richard replied, and again there was that hint of innuendo that unsettled her.

Catherine led Ambrosia into a stall and clipped cross ties to her halter to discourage the pony from her irritating habit of reaching around to nip the backside of whoever groomed her. She quickly checked the pony's hooves, then reached for a brush and started working with firm, brisk strokes. Maybe he'd take the hint and leave her alone if she just kept about her business.

"When do you have time off?" he asked.

"Time off?" She shrugged, continuing to work. "There's always something to do, especially during tournament time."

"Meet me for dinner tonight. You can tell me more about yourself."

Was he so sure of himself that he didn't even couch his invitation as a question? She should have been irritated by his assurance but, perversely, she felt a sudden tingle of excitement ripple through her. A thoroughly unwelcome tingle.

"Sorry, I can't. I'm too busy."

She felt the air between them move, solidify. Then the warm pressure of his hand over hers, his fingers tangling with her own over the brush she held against the pony's flank. An electric sizzle of awareness tracked up her arm and through her body. The heat of him behind her suffused the too-thin fabric of her polo shirt, making her all too aware of his nearness—his very maleness. She held herself rigid to prevent herself from leaning back against that all too enticing wall of confidence and strength he projected.

"People don't usually refuse me," he said, his lips suddenly altogether too close to her ear.

She slid her hand out from beneath his and ducked under Ambrosia's neck to start brushing her other side while she fought to control a heartbeat that was too rapid. She knew her cheeks would be flushed, a curse of her fair skin, and she swallowed before replying.

"Sounds like it's past time you got used to that, then."

Catherine bit the inside of her cheek, forcing herself not to respond any further. She was not normally this blunt, nor was she usually averse to dinner with a handsome man. But Richard Wells was off-limits, no matter how much he pinged every sensor in her body. Wealthy, entitled and, above all, totally out of her league. No. She did not want to go down that path.

His sudden burst of laughter made her startle, causing Ambrosia to shift again, this time landing one well-shod hoof firmly on top of Catherine's boot. She bit back a curse and pushed against the pony, extricating her foot.

"C'mon," Richard cajoled, "it's only dinner."

"Why on earth would you want to have dinner with me? You don't even know me."

He looked at her. Catherine felt her breasts tighten as his gaze flicked over her body before settling on her face.

"We could change that."

Her mouth dried, and the words she knew she should

utter to stop him once and for all hovered, for the moment, unsaid on her lips. His clear, gray eyes bored into hers, mesmerizing her with the intent mirrored there.

"No."

She was adamant. She simply wasn't going there.

"At least tell me your name," he coaxed.

"Catherine," she replied, her voice a little husky. "Catherine Lawson."

"Well, Catherine Lawson, I'm Richard Wells, and I'm *very* pleased to meet you."

"I know who you are," she answered, ignoring the hand he'd thrust out over Ambrosia's back in a parody of a formal introduction.

She wasn't letting him touch her again—no way. He affected her too darn much for her to risk that. The last thing she wanted was to be linked to him this season. She knew full well how the taint of scandal clung to a person and how damaging the fallout was for the weaker parties involved.

No. No matter how enticing, Richard Wells would remain firmly out of bounds.

Two

"Your admirer is here again."

Catherine stifled a groan and fought the urge to scan the fence around the field where they were doing stick and ball practice with the sheikh's top string of ponies for the major tournament starting in six weeks. But she couldn't help herself—she looked. Dressed in a silky black shirt and designer jeans, Richard leaned casually against the fence, his eyes shaded by a ball cap. They might be shaded, she thought, but his eyes were very firmly upon her, if the prickle between her shoulder blades was anything to go by.

Didn't he have better things to do than to shadow her on a daily basis? Every day for a week he'd either turned up at the stables, helping out as if he were a groom and not some gold-edged, white-collared multibillionaire, or had come to watch her on the fields during practice.

Every day he asked her to dinner again, and every day she turned him down.

She would not turn and look at him. She. Would. Not.

She looked.

Her heart skipped a beat. It was bad enough that he invaded her waking thoughts, but now he filled her sleeping ones, as well, and last night had been a doozy. She'd woken before dawn, drenched in sweat, her sheets in a tangle and her body humming with a longing that just wouldn't go away. A longing that never got the chance to go away with him standing there, watching her, day after day. Clearly the word "no" simply meant "try harder" for men like Richard Wells.

Her grooms bore the brunt of her frustration. Each day's chores were more meticulously supervised than they had been the day before. Each time a pony's legs were bandaged in preparation for practice, they were more carefully examined and checked before being deemed to be okay. Tack had to be in pristine condition before being returned to the tack room.

She knew she was being a pain, but she couldn't help it. Richard Wells had her so wound up she could barely think straight. She was doing her best to hold firm, but somehow her best simply wasn't quite enough to ensure a good night's sleep anymore.

On top of everything, this afternoon, instead of working the pony lines and supervising her grooms, she'd been summoned to make an appearance in the sheikh's VIP tent. It seemed that the ponies had garnered the attention of some overseas interest, and the people involved wanted to meet her, as well. Why, she had no idea. Sheikh Adham Aal Ferjani was as hands-on as his work allowed. It was one of the things that she most respected about him. He wasn't a figurehead, but an integral part of the process of bringing his polo ponies up to the standards he demanded in play. He expected the same level of commitment from all his team members, no matter their worldwide ranking. The sheikh was more than capable of fielding any and all enquiries about his horses.

Catherine loathed the idea of having to wear a dress, heels and makeup and make polite conversation with the kind of people who usually set her teeth on edge. The social side of polo had never been her scene. Which was another reason why she and a man like Richard Wells could never amount to anything together.

No, his type would be more like the sycophantic designer-clad hordes who deluged the Hamptons with their perfect hair and their perfect smiles and their perfect clothes. Catherine gave herself a mental shake. She wasn't being entirely fair. Sure, as with any endeavor steeped in tradition and money, there were those who were only there to see and be seen, but there were just as many with a genuine interest and love of the sport.

She'd let Richard Wells get too far under her skin, she decided as she called a halt to the practice session and led her team back to the barn. Or maybe, a sneaky little voice inside her suggested, she hadn't allowed him under her skin quite deep enough.

As soon as she'd thought it, a sharply edged visual image painted itself in her mind, and her inner muscles clenched tight. A tiny moan escaped from her lips as a surge of longing swelled deep within her.

"Are you okay?" one of her grooms asked as he drew alongside her.

Catherine felt her cheeks flame at the prospect of his having heard her.

"I'm fine. Just not looking forward to this afternoon, is all."

"Hey, you'll be in the shade, drinking champagne and rubbing shoulders with the powers that be. What's not to like?"

"All of the above?" she managed, with a wry smile.

The other groom laughed and dismounted his horse, leading it into the barn ahead of her. Catherine reached up to unclip her helmet and remove it. Sometimes she wished she could be more like some of her grooms. Most of them were much younger than her twenty-eight years and, for them, relationships came and went and were purely to be enjoyed. Many were working solely for the experience and to have a chance to increase their rankings, hopefully with a view of catching the eye of a wealthy patron who would boost their polo playing career into the stratosphere.

But Catherine's dreams lay in other areas. A natural left-hander, she'd trained herself as competently as any right-handed player—doing so had been vital to her being able to do her job well. But even so, her heart wasn't in the game itself. No, her heart lay firmly and squarely with the horses, and she wanted nothing more than to establish her own riding stables. A pipe dream at the best of times, unless she could secure some serious sponsorship to get her ideas off the ground. But she hoped to one day be able to provide riding lessons to kids from underprivileged backgrounds as well as those who could afford to pay for the pleasure.

"Penny for them?"

Richard's voice dragged her attention firmly back to where it belonged.

"Not even worth that, unfortunately," she replied,

swinging her leg over and dropping from her saddle to the yard floor.

"So, about dinner…"

She'd had enough. Catherine handed her pony off to one of the other grooms with a short command and turned to give Richard her full attention.

"I thought I made it perfectly clear. I'm not interested in having dinner with you."

"If I gave up every time I heard the word *no,* I wouldn't be where I am today."

He smiled at her, the action softening the sharp planes of his face and lending a lighter, more boyish, cast to his features. She fought the natural instinct to smile in return, instead focusing on a point just past his ear.

"It's not going to happen."

"Why not?"

"Because I'm not interested in you."

"So, then, you have nothing to lose, do you?"

"I also have nothing to gain, either."

"Good point. Okay, so back to the not interested thing. I've learned to be a pretty good judge of a person's character and to read visual cues that most people don't realize they're sending out."

He crossed his arms and took his time to peruse her from the soles of her boots to the top of her helmet.

"Frankly," he said, "I don't believe you."

Catherine huffed out a breath in frustration. "I really don't care if you believe me or not. Look, let me put it this way. There's no way I'm going to be your summer fling. We're from completely different backgrounds, completely different worlds. All I care about is horses, not people, so please stop wasting your time and go ask someone who might actually say yes."

"I don't recall asking you to be my summer fling, although the idea has merit."

He let his gaze drift over her face, his eyes fixing on her lips and making her think twice about her sudden urge to run her tongue across them.

"Catherine, it's just a meal. Shared between two adults."

His subtle emphasis on the word *adults* sent a pull through her body as visceral as if he'd reached out and stroked the full length of her. She gathered her scattered wits and juggled the words in her mind.

"The answer is still, and will continue to be, no. Now, please, I have work to do."

Richard watched Catherine as she straightened her shoulders and walked away, every step of her booted feet resonating on the yard surface and echoing her displeasure. Why was he being so persistent? It wasn't as if he was hard-pressed for female company. Ah, but not company who challenged him. And not company who wouldn't expect more than he was prepared to give.

He'd kept the news of the final dissolution of his marriage quiet for a darn good reason and thanked the perspicacity of his lawyer for insisting on a gag clause to prevent Daniella from leaking the information. He wasn't being narcissistic when he said he knew he was fair game on the marriage market. He was passably good-looking, fit, still young and financially healthy— very healthy. He had no desire to suddenly be the object of several hundred single—and some not-so-single— women looking for their next alimony check. No. He'd made that mistake once, and he wasn't about to do it again.

When he sought female company from now on it

would be entirely on his terms, which was why he was so determined to win Catherine over. Physically, she was as different from Daniella as night from day. Her lean, lightly muscled limbs were a far cry from his ex-wife's voluptuous curves and shorter frame. He clenched his hands into fists as he imagined how Catherine's body would feel beneath him, how her lithe limbs would entangle with his, how her slim hips would cradle his own, how her pert small breasts would feel in his hands, beneath his tongue….

Fire licked through his body, starting at the soles of his feet and roaring through him, setting every nerve into full aching arousal. If just thinking about making love with her did this to him, what would the real thing be like? He genuinely looked forward to finding out. That it would take relentless chipping at the hard granite of her determination to refuse him just sweetened the deal.

Damn, she was stubborn. And he liked stubborn. Richard hadn't yet met a challenge he couldn't coerce into submission, and Catherine's submission was something he was very much looking forward to. In fact, the harder she worked to dissuade him, the more certain he became he'd succeed. And he'd ensure it was totally worth her while to capitulate. Totally.

Richard turned and headed back to the guesthouse. He needed a long, cold shower before he got ready for watching the matches this afternoon. A very long, very cold shower.

Three

Richard strolled among the crowds as people bustled and gossiped around the VIP tents at the polo field. Hard to believe some were even here to watch the games, he thought with a touch of cynicism. To his eye, it appeared that most spectators were interested in being seen by the right people. But then that was all part and parcel of the sport, he conceded as he greeted one of his colleagues from the city.

Seb had introduced him today to Catherine's boss, Sheikh Adham Aal Ferjani. Richard had liked the man instantly and had been intrigued by the fact that his dark eyes had never strayed far from his beautiful, but somewhat quiet, wife. He knew she'd suffered a family bereavement recently. Perhaps that explained her husband's ever-watchful gaze.

Over near the entrance to the tents, paparazzi were scrambling for the best shot of newly arrived Carmen

Akins. The award-winning actress was even more beautiful in the flesh than on screen, although there was a tense set to her mouth. Security was quick to step in and prevent the mob from following her any farther, however.

And there was Vanessa Hughes, wearing her trademark white designer gear and black-rimmed sunglasses that almost obscured her face, and carrying the voluminous bag he knew contained the flat-heeled shoes she preferred to wear to stomp the divots at half-time despite the fact they reduced her to her very petite five foot two. He'd always loved her for her practicality in this if nothing else. She smiled and waved before her attention was caught by a mutual friend.

He wondered how Catherine was faring. The busyness of the pony lines was a far cry from the circus of people and behaviors in the tents, he was certain. No doubt it was vastly preferable, too.

Richard took a sip of his champagne and scanned the assembly, his gaze flitting over his companions before halting in surprise on one particular face.

Catherine. A very dressed up and elegant Catherine at that. Her hair had been pulled back from her face, and instead of the usual wisps slipping from the loose braid that usually hung down her back, every strand was firmly secured into an elegant knot at her nape. A deliciously exposed nape. A nape made for nuzzling, he thought with a smile.

The severe style suited her, revealing her smooth forehead and high cheekbones to perfection. A small silver ring pierced the top of her right ear, her only jewelry. She wore barely any makeup, but he could tell she'd applied some mascara and probably some foundation, as the faint freckles that so intrigued him each day were smoothly obscured. A slick shiny tint on her lips was just about his undoing, however. If she'd been here as his partner there was no way she'd still have that on. It would've been kissed off quite thoroughly by now.

He saw the exact moment she registered his perusal of her, her eyes flicking across him, her body stiffening, her smile becoming forced. And beneath the filmy fabric of the dress she wore he could swear he saw her nipples tighten and bud against the teal-green cloth that gave her eyes a hint of the sea. A stormy sea, if that tense jaw was anything to go by.

This was the first time he'd seen her in anything other than riding breeches, boots and a polo shirt. He liked this side of her—a lot. Always graceful and regal on horseback, she was even more so clad in the simple but elegant dress that clung lovingly to her body. The knee-length dress showcased her lower legs and a very slender, fine turn of ankle. Even her feet looked beautiful in stylish heeled sandals. Nothing ostentatious—just simple, quiet chic.

She'd painted her toenails a soft, peachy pink that went well with her skin tone. He had to admit surprise that she'd even bother with such frippery when she spent most of her time in boots anyway. It only served to remind him how little he really knew about Catherine Lawson—and how very much he wanted to know more.

He smiled to himself again and turned slightly away from her. She knew he was here. It would be interesting to see whether or not she'd come talk to him. He'd wager not.

The next game was due to commence, and people had begun to filter out of the tent. Richard decided to follow Catherine, perhaps even take a place next to her as they watched the game, but the sound of her name made him pause.

"Isn't that Catherine Lawson, Del Lawson's girl?" asked a tall slender blonde of her equally slender and glamorously attired companion.

"Del Lawson? Wasn't he linked to that doping scandal in New Zealand years ago?"

Just ahead of him, Richard noticed Catherine's shoulders stiffen and her step falter.

"The sheikh had better look after his ponies if she's working for him," the first blonde commented.

"They do say the apple never falls far from the tree," her cohort said and laughed snidely as they continued with their champagne glasses out to the main spectator area.

Richard edged his way through the exiting crowd, suddenly desperate to get to Catherine's side. There was no way she hadn't heard the two women discussing her. He'd seen the way she'd reacted. He scanned the crowd for the kingfisher flash of teal fabric, but he couldn't see her anywhere.

Then he caught sight of her, past the VIP tents and heading in the direction of the pony lines. Every inch of her body was held taut and straight, and he could almost see the waves of distress pouring off her. He followed, suddenly filled with the overwhelming desire to protect her. He knew he couldn't undo what she'd heard, but he could get to the root of what had upset her—and then maybe he could make things right for her again.

Richard didn't question the unexpected and un-characteristic urge to shield and defend a woman who was still essentially a stranger to him. All he knew was that she was upset and, come hell or high water, he was going to fix that.

Catherine blinked back the burn of tears that ached at the back of her eyes. She would not cry. She refused to let the cattiness of a couple of strangers break through the wall she'd spent the last twelve years shoring up around her. Who'd have believed that a handful of words, carelessly spoken, could still have the capacity to reach into her heart and claw it open like this?

She tripped, one of her high heels catching on the uneven ground, but she steadied herself and kept going, desperate to create some distance between herself and the aching pain of the past.

"Catherine. Catherine. Stop."

Warm hands caught her arms, forcing her to a halt. Even as Richard's voice registered, she struggled to pull free.

"Let me go."

"No. I won't let you go."

His hands slid up her arms to her shoulders and turned her around before pulling her into the warm heat of his body. She knew she ought to push him away, that she shouldn't find instant, gratifying comfort against the hard plane of his chest. That the feel of his arms, looped across her back and holding her fast, shouldn't make her feel as if she wasn't totally and completely alone in the world.

She couldn't help it. The tears she'd been fighting so hard to hold back began to slide inexorably down her cheeks. She sniffed, then felt Richard shift slightly before he pressed a clean, white handkerchief into her hands. He only let her go long enough to blow her nose and dab futilely at the moisture on her face before gathering her close again.

Slowly she felt the tension begin to ease from her back and shoulders. Her body sank into his as if he were the only thing holding her upright. Wiping at her face one more time, Catherine pulled away.

"Thank you, I think," she said shakily. "I'll, um, get this back to you once it's been laundered." She gestured to the wadded fist of cotton in her hand.

"Don't worry about it. Are you okay now?"

"Yeah."

She turned her face away, hardly able to bear his scrutiny. She never, never let go like this in front of anyone. Since she was sixteen, she'd essentially been on her own. Estranged from her mother. Her father dead. She'd learned to stand on her own two feet. Losing control like this, especially with someone like Richard Wells, was anathema to her. She dredged up the steel mantle under which she usually maintained control.

It was stupid to have reacted that way to those women's throwaway remarks. She'd heard worse over the years, words that had far more capacity to hurt than any aspersion on her own character.

Richard stood a mere foot away from her, watching her, poised as if to shelter her from harm. The sensation that someone else was looking out for her was foreign but strangely alluring. And dangerous—way too dangerous.

"You want to talk about it?" he asked.

"No," she responded flatly. Run, hide, escape—yes. Talking about it was the last thing she wanted to do.

"Do you have to go back?" he asked, his eyes not leaving her face.

"Go back?" she answered, momentarily confused.

"To the tents."

"No. No, I did my thing. The sheikh has some potential buyers for some of the ponies. They wanted to meet me, too."

"Can I walk you? Or would you rather we drove?"

Catherine shook her head. "No, I'll be fine. I was going to go to the pony lines, check that everything's okay and then head back to my apartment."

"I'll come with you."

"That's not necessary. I don't need you to hold my hand."

"I know. You're tough and brave—you don't need anybody, do you?"

Richard studied her carefully. Catherine felt her eyes widen as the shock of his words hit home. Was that what he really thought about her? That she didn't need anybody?

He couldn't be more wrong. She ached to belong to someone, someone who wouldn't judge her for who she was or where she'd come from. Someone who wouldn't look down their nose at her because she didn't have a university degree. Someone who would understand that while horses were her life, she still needed that special person in her world to make her complete. A man who could help her reach for the stars yet keep her grounded in the security of his love.

"I bet you don't know what it feels like to be constantly rejected," he said. A twinkle of amusement in his slate-colored eyes gave the lie to the implied hurt in his words.

She couldn't help it. She laughed, the sound bubbling up in her throat to chase away the lingering sorrow and bitterness left by the comments she'd overhead in the VIP tent.

"Are you talking about yourself now?" she teased lightly.

"Of course I am."

"I doubt you've ever been soundly rejected in your whole life."

"You've rejected me. It's left me wounded."

She laughed again. "You're kidding me. Men like you—you're so tough. You just move on to the next conquest, don't you?"

He didn't respond immediately, but his expression changed a little.

"Is that how you see me?"

Catherine's breath caught in her throat. Had she offended him? So close on the heels of the kindness he'd just shown her, that was the last thing she'd wanted to do.

"I..." Words dried on her tongue.

"Go on. Ask me on a date and I'll show you what it feels like."

"What? You want me to ask *you* on a date?"

"That's the idea."

"And you'll say no, so I know how it feels to be rejected? No, thanks. I know. Trust me on this."

"I'd never have figured you for a coward," he goaded with a smile on his face that went all the way to his eyes, crinkling the corners with devilish mirth.

"Oh, all right, then." Catherine gave a long-suffering sigh. "Would you like to go out with me sometime?"

"Love to. Where and when?"

Her heart slammed into her chest. The sneak! He'd tricked her into asking him out, and she'd fallen for it. Hook, line and sinker. Now she felt as if she'd just reined in a half-broken stallion but had no idea what to do next.

"That's not fair. I didn't mean it. You made me ask you under false pretences," she backpedaled.

"Catherine, you need to learn something about me. When I want something, I will get it eventually. Even if it means going a different, or less conventional, route."

He smiled at her again, but this time there was no guile in his expression. This was the determined, hardheaded businessman who'd co-founded an internationally successful media company with Sebastian Hughes, without a single ounce of assistance from anyone else.

She should be annoyed—very annoyed. Yet deep down there was a piece of her that was glad he'd said yes, despite their very obvious differences. But what on earth could she do with a man like Richard Wells who was used to the best of everything—restaurants, cars, people?

How could she, a groom, expect to compete with the dates he was used to? Every penny she made she tried to save for her own stables. She was lucky that in the course of her work she was provided with accommodation and Sheik Adham was generous with allowances for riding gear, but she still had a ways to go to reach her goal.

Would Richard be satisfied with something simple? And why did she even care? He'd tricked her into this date. It would serve him right if it was something he didn't expect or enjoy.

Something her father used to say to her when she was young echoed from the back of her mind. *You can tell a lot about a man by the way he treats a horse.* Perfect. Suddenly she knew exactly what they'd be doing.

"Fine." Catherine nodded. "Meet me at the barn tomorrow morning at sunup. Wear riding gear, if you have any."

"That's it? We're going for a ride?"

"Hey, you asked me where and when. Consider yourself told. If you stand me up, I won't come looking for you."

"Don't worry, I'll be there. You can count on it."

Richard turned and walked back toward the polo field. As she watched him go, Catherine wondered if perhaps she hadn't bitten off more than she could chew. Richard Wells outclassed her, outmaneuvered her and, quite simply, took her breath away.

Four

It was a morning just like any other morning, Catherine reminded herself. Chores to do, horses to attend to, notes to make for the vet who'd be calling in a few hours to check the ponies already under his care after the hardships of yesterday's games.

And yet, it was a morning unlike any other, too. Bubbles of anticipation popped and fizzed in her stomach. Anticipation tinged with a healthy dose of nerves. She'd barely been able to sleep last night and had fully intended to leave a message with the Hugheses' housekeeping staff to tell Richard she couldn't make it today. But despite the fact she knew he wouldn't let her off so lightly, there was a part of her that looked forward to this time alone with him, as well.

"Pathetic," she growled at herself as she tacked up two of her favorite horses for the early morning ride. Both were gentle in nature because she had no idea how comfortable Richard would be on horseback, and she didn't want to put him in a position where he might be embarrassed. Although she doubted that embarrassment occurred very often in his world.

Even though she'd braided her hair back in its customary single rope, tendrils already escaped to kiss the sides of her neck and face. A shiver rippled down her spine. It was more than the sensation of a drift of hair across bare skin. He was here. She knew it as surely as she knew her own face in the mirror each morning. Catherine didn't hasten in checking the girth strap and adjusting the stirrup leathers of the mount she'd chosen for herself. Eventually, though, she knew she'd have to face him.

She gave her horse a final pat and turned around. The instant she did, the sensation she'd felt only seconds ago sharpened and honed in on her chest, squeezing the air out of her lungs. She'd suspected he wasn't unfamiliar with horses, but you could never assume anything in the privileged world in which she worked.

He looked the part, from the polo shirt he'd topped with a sleeveless jacket to the well-worn boots on his feet. That his gear was anything but for show was obvious. The fitted leather boots hugged his calves, and his breeches followed the taut line of his thighs and hips with near-sinful intimacy. A riding helmet dangled from his fingers—again, well used and more for function than for show.

She could only imagine how good he'd look in the saddle, those powerful thighs nudging his horse on, reins comfortably held between his long fingers. Catherine swallowed against the sudden dryness in her throat.

"Good morning," he said. "I take it you were serious about going for a ride?"

Even his smile was enough to set her nerves skittering throughout her body.

"You gather correctly," she managed to reply far more evenly than she'd expected. She gestured to his gear. "I take it you can ride. Maybe you'd like a mount a bit more spirited than old Gryphon here," she said, patting the tall but docile gray gelding on the rump.

"Not today. Today I want to concentrate on you. In fact," he said as he opened one side of his jacket to show his cell phone tucked in a purpose-made pocket, "my phone is even on silent."

His eyes met and dueled with hers, making it impossible to look away. As he smiled again, she noted the way the corners of his eyes fanned softly, as if smiling were a natural thing for him. She supposed he had little to worry about. Raised on money, making his own money—what was there to concern him on a daily basis besides stock values and who his next escort would be?

Richard broke the contact himself and stepped over to Gryphon, taking a moment to say hello to the horse.

"I think Gryphon and I will get along just fine. Besides, it's been a while since I've had the time to ride. It'll be good to relax and enjoy the scenery."

He flashed her another look that left her in no doubt as to what "scenery" he referred to. For a second—a split second, no more—she allowed herself to preen just a little under his regard. To believe that she was the kind of woman who attracted a man like Richard Wells for real, not just for some passing fancy, which was all this could ever be.

"Well, then. We'd better head out and enjoy some of that scenery," she said, sliding her foot into a stirrup and pulling herself up onto her saddle. "There's rain forecast for later today. I'm hoping it'll hold off for now."

Richard quickly checked his stirrup leathers then followed suit. Together they rode out of the yard and down the lane that led away from the main farm buildings.

Catherine found herself enjoying the companionable silence between them although she kept wondering what it really was that made Richard tick. He hadn't let up on her for a second since he'd been at Seven Oaks. Even the days he'd been at the games he'd sought her out, and if he hadn't caught her at the pony lines, he'd found her later in the evening exercising the horses that hadn't been played.

She hated to admit it to herself, but she'd come to look forward to seeing him every day. Every day but yesterday, she reminded herself. She certainly hadn't needed him to witness either the shaming remarks those women had so casually thrown out like a discarded handbag or her reaction to them. Over the years she'd taught herself to cope so much better than that, but knowing Richard had heard them had lent an even more bitter tang to the encounter. She wondered if he'd made it his business to find out about the scandal that had ultimately led to her father's death.

She was such a fool for letting him trick her into this date. She'd chosen to take him riding thinking, wrongly, that it would give her the upper hand. But if the way he sat Gryphon was any indicator, he was probably as at home in a saddle as he was at the head of a boardroom table in the city.

The sun was a little higher in the sky now, filtering through gathering clouds, and the birdsong around them grew louder as they approached a tall stand of trees.

"Want to stretch him out a bit?" she asked as she bent to unlatch the gate they'd ridden up to.

"I thought you'd never ask," Richard replied, guiding his horse through the open gate and waiting for her on the other side. As she pulled up alongside him, he nodded to a solitary tree silhouetted against the rising sun. "Race you."

"You're on," Catherine answered after relatching the gate.

Without a second thought, she urged her mount forward. Gryphon was fast, but he wasn't quite as fleet of foot as her own horse, which required very little urging to stretch out into a full gallop. The sound of two sets of hooves thundering across the ground rang in her ears as they raced toward their goal.

If only life could always be this simple, she thought briefly before reminding herself to just relish the moment instead. Laughter began to bubble from her throat as she edged ahead of Richard and his horse, pulling up in the lead and reaching the tree a few seconds ahead of him.

"You're good," she acknowledged. "Not everyone can get that much speed out of him."

Richard patted Gryphon's strong neck before replying. "We reached an understanding."

"That's quite an understanding." Catherine smiled in return.

"Oh, I'm pretty amenable to most things. Clearly Gryphon and I are similar in that regard."

They resumed their trek side by side across the field in silence. Surprisingly for Catherine it was very comfortable just being with Richard. If anything, perhaps it was a bit too comfortable. She could get used to this kind of companionable closeness all too easily. But she knew this was only a short-lived stint in the countryside for him. His world was the city and its teeming busyness of life and work there. Her world, such as it was, was quite different.

Richard sensed Catherine's mood had changed. Somehow she'd slipped from carefree to quiet introspection and was withdrawing from him emotionally. He knew he'd surprised her by coming down in his riding gear. No doubt she'd expected him to be more like the rest of the guests staying at Seven Oaks and in neighboring compounds—only there for the society and the games and whatever peripheral activities they entailed.

He drew in a deep breath. Man, he'd give up working in the city if every day could be like this. He knew Seb's time here was bittersweet with the worry about his father's illness and the additional responsibilities he'd had to take on, but to be able to live this life— complementary to their usual world—would be the perfect marriage of ideals.

Catherine pulled up ahead of him, beside one of several ponds on the property. Her eyes fixed on the serene smoothness of the water. She was a lot like that herself, he realized. Calm on the surface, yet who knew what hidden depths she veiled from view? Suddenly, he was sick of playing the game he'd played with her for days now. He wasn't the kind of man to wait for someone else to make the first move. And he knew Catherine would run a mile before admitting she found him even moderately attractive.

He let his eyes drift over her as she sat so perfectly in her saddle. Her figure was lithe and strong, and he woke each morning consumed with the desire to know how she'd feel beneath his touch. Would she be shy, or reserved? Or would she take control and ride him as effortlessly as she became a part of the horses that were her charge?

He drew his mount alongside hers. They were so close that their legs brushed against one another. She turned to him, distracted from her reveries, and he knew exactly what he had to do next. Leaning over, he reached for her and cupped the back of her neck with one hand to draw her closer.

He absorbed the scent of her, fresh and clean, with a hint of lemon and mint—none of the cloying sweetness or spice of so many of the fragrances women wore. Nothing but the essence of her. He'd never smelled anything more enticing.

Her lips parted to protest, but he pressed his mouth to hers. She froze, rigid beside him, as his lips teased hers, as he supped and tasted their softness—a softness in direct contrast with the strength of her body and the steel will he sensed drove her to be who she was.

Fire leaped in his veins, licking at his insides, burning him up with a heat he knew could only be quenched by one thing, one woman. He slid his tongue along her lower lip and felt a thrill of triumph as it trembled at his touch. He'd half expected her to pull away, but instead she leaned in closer, appearing to want to absorb him as much as he wanted her.

He couldn't get enough. He deepened the kiss, letting his tongue slide between her lips to claim hers. The fire inside him turned molten, his thoughts and awareness flowing with the inexorable slow heat of a river of lava.

Sound retreated, leaving only sensation—and what sensation. All he was doing was kissing her. But no, this was so much more. This was a total communion of spirit.

He sucked gently on her full lower lip one more time before releasing her.

"You're beautiful, you know that?" he said, his voice low and steady.

Catherine shook her head. "You don't have to lie to me."

He lifted his hand and took her chin with strong fingers, making her look him directly in the eye. How could she not know how stunning she was, how she affected him on every level?

"I don't make a habit of lying, Catherine. You are beautiful. Always remember that."

She opened her mouth as if to protest, but the gathering clouds chose that moment to open and let the full weight of the moisture they carried fall pell-mell to the ground.

"Oh, no, I was hoping that would hold off until we got back," Catherine said, gathering her reins and turning her horse away from the pond. "There's an old barn not too far away. It'll be closer than heading back to the main farm. We can shelter there until the rain stops."

Without waiting for him to reply, she urged her horse forward, leaving him with nothing to do but follow her. Gryphon appeared equally motivated to get out of the weather as quickly as he could, Richard noticed. He wondered whether the downpour would be at all effective in cooling his ardor.

Catherine had dismounted and was wrestling two large doors open, the rain plastering her lightweight shirt to her skin, outlining her bra in intimate detail. He shouldn't feel so aroused—it wasn't as if the practical cotton garment had been designed to entice and titillate—but the sight of it only served to increase his growing hunger for its wearer.

The rain grew even heavier. Richard slid from his saddle and splashed through the rapidly growing puddles to help Catherine maneuver the doors open. Together they swung the massive doors wide and led their horses into the barn before pulling the doors closed behind them. While Richard secured them from the inside, Catherine led the horses to a couple of empty stalls and tethered them inside before loosening their girth straps and giving them each a bucket of water.

Richard took off his helmet and looked around the barn. It was old but seemed to be kept in very good condition, and he said as much to Catherine.

"I believe Mr. Hughes uses it as an overflow barn from time to time during tournaments. Saves other teams from having to transport their horses in. This time, though, the sheikh requested exclusive use of the farm." She shivered slightly. "There must be blankets or towels around here somewhere."

Richard followed her as she went to what looked like a small tack room off to one side of the barn. The room was pretty bare—a sagging sofa along one wall, a small wooden table pushed against another and one small window set high up, beneath which was an array of empty pegs and hooks for holding the various saddlery and tack for the horses. Dust motes spun in the sparse, watery light cast through the window.

He shucked off his jacket and tossed it across the table while Catherine riffled through a cupboard. If he was any kind of gentleman he'd avert his eyes from her almost completely transparent shirt, but right now manners were the furthest thing from his mind.

Outside, the rain battered the curved roof of the

barn with increasing ferocity, and the light inside the tack room dimmed even more. They were cocooned in here, safe from the elements, but not at all safe from the elemental need that coursed through his veins.

"Here, use this to dry yourself off a bit," Catherine said, passing him a towel.

"What about you?"

"I'll dry off after you."

She shivered again, a delicate ripple of muscle over bone.

"Here, let me help you. You look as though you need it more than me."

Truth be told, he should be steaming he felt so warm right now. Without waiting for Catherine's response, he unclipped her helmet, his fingers grazing the soft skin at her throat. He tossed the helmet onto the tabletop and gently wiped the moisture from her face and, turning her away from him, wrapped her braid in the thin towel to squeeze the water from her hair.

"The towel's going to be useless after that," she commented, her voice a little unsteady.

"Yeah," he agreed, his fingers already sliding the band off the end of her braid and rapidly loosening her hair.

"What are you doing?"

"It'll dry faster like this. Besides, I've always wanted to see your hair out."

"I'll look like a hairy drowned rat."

A smile pulled at his lips. "You look beautiful, remember?"

He turned her to face him and traced the shape of one brow with a finger.

"Beautiful," he said, his voice suddenly thick with need.

He bent his head and kissed her again, pulling her to

him, letting her slight frame nestle damply against his. Another tremor rocked her, but this time he doubted it was from the cold. Her lips burned against his, and he could feel the points of her nipples harden against his chest as they pressed through the thin fabric of her bra.

"I want to see you. All of you," he whispered against her lips.

He thought for a moment she'd refuse. Felt her denial building in the air between them. But then she nodded. Just the slightest inclination of her head.

He ran his hands down her back to the hem of her shirt and lightly tugged it upward, relinquishing her lips for long enough to pull the sodden garment over her head and let it drop to the floor. A flick of his wrist and her bra was undone. Slowly, almost reverently, he peeled the straps off her shoulders and down her arms, exposing her small, high breasts to his touch. He brushed her pale pink nipples lightly with his fingertips, feeling them tighten even more beneath his touch, before tracing her ribs and the gentle curve of her waist.

Carefully he backed her against the table before bending to remove her boots and socks and finally her riding breeches and panties. As he straightened, so did she, standing there before him, slender and proud. His for the taking. He felt as if he'd been waiting for this moment all his life. And he sure as hell wasn't about to let it pass him by.

Five

Catherine had never felt as bold as she did right now standing naked before Richard. There was a look of awe on his face as his eyes roamed her body, and she felt his gaze as if it were a physical flame warming her from the inside out.

He made her feel beautiful. Strong. Female.

She watched as he seemed to come to his senses, bending to remove his boots, followed quickly by the rest of his clothing. And there he stood opposite her. Completely naked but for a smattering of dark hair at the center of his chest. A smattering that narrowed into a fine line and arrowed down past his belly button. Her fingers itched to trace it, to touch him—taste him.

He'd said she was beautiful, but she could just as easily have said the same of him. There wasn't a visible ounce of fat on his body. He was lean, sculpted muscle from the breadth of his shoulders all the way to his calves. She reached out to touch him and felt his skin shiver slightly beneath her fingertips as she did so. She trailed her fingers lightly across his shoulders and down over his pectoral muscles before circling his small dark brown nipples.

Obeying her body's demands, she bent her head to flick her tongue over one taut disk and was rewarded with a barely suppressed groan. Richard's hands reached out and tangled in the long, loose strands of her hair as he pulled her closer to him, aligning her body against his.

He was so hard and hot—everywhere. His erection was trapped between them and feeling his solid length made her move against him, eager to assuage the ache that gathered from deep inside. She lifted one leg, hooked it across his hip and angled her pelvis so his hardness sent tiny shock waves spiraling out from her center.

One moment she'd been cold and chilled, the next she was an inferno of need. For a split second, she hesitated. She couldn't believe she was here. With him. Doing this. But then his warmth enveloped her as her body burned against his and his arms closed around her back, his hands spread against her skin. Any thought of hesitation, of stopping and recovering her sanity, was utterly lost. There was time enough later to worry about the self-recriminations that would come, but now, right now, she wanted Richard with a need that went bone deep.

His hands coasted down her back and over her buttocks, pulling her even closer against him. She tilted her hips again, back and forth, desperate to relieve some of the demanding pressure at her core that begged to be assuaged. It wasn't enough but it would do for now, and she both heard and felt the purr of satisfaction that rippled uncontrollably from her throat.

"So you like that, do you?" Richard nuzzled against her neck.

She flexed again and nodded, words completely failing her as sharp points of pleasure zapped through her. Richard stifled a groan, the vibration of the sound against the tender skin at her throat initiating its own drumbeat of want. His hands gripped her buttocks tighter, lifting her higher.

"Put your other leg around me," he instructed, his voice little more than a growl.

Catherine did as he bade and, holding her with one hand, he quickly spread out his jacket across the table's surface and lowered her onto the dry, quilted lining. She hissed in a breath as the cool skin of her buttocks settled against the lingering warmth of his body that remained in the silky fabric beneath her. She locked her ankles behind him, loath to lose the delicious sensations that cascaded through her at their point of contact.

"Lean back a little," he said.

Catherine transferred her weight to her hands, spreading her fingers against the tabletop. A tiny mew of protest fled her throat as he unhooked her feet and let them dangle down, her legs splayed.

He took his time, watching her carefully as he ran his hands up her legs, softly massaging her calves, gently tracing behind her knees and stroking firmly over her thighs toward the small nest of curls at their apex. Catherine sucked her lower lip in between her teeth and caught it fast as his fingers teased—circling ever closer, yet not touching the point that burned for him.

Richard leaned forward and flicked one nipple, then

the other, with his tongue. A groan ripped from her throat as he simultaneously palmed her heated entrance. She thrust against him and groaned again as he took one nipple in his mouth, suckling hard, rasping the tender flesh with the edge of his teeth, then laving it gently with his tongue once more.

He was driving her crazy.

Crazy with need.

Crazy for him.

She felt his fingers stroke the folds of skin at the entrance to her body, felt him part them, then slide one finger inside her. Her hips took up a slow undulating rhythm of their own as she strived to reach the ephemeral peak his touch promised.

"Ah, you taste so sweet," he said, transferring his attention to her other nipple. "You have no idea how many times I've imagined doing this to you."

Words failed her as he slid his thumb over her, stroking and pressing against the hooded pearl in time with the rise and fall of her hips. She was so close. So very close. Any second now and she'd fracture apart.

Her arms began to shake, and she felt him withdraw his hand from her body.

"Don't stop. Please, don't stop now," she all but begged, her voice a foreign sound to her ears.

"Don't worry, I have no intention of stopping."

Through the glaze of desire in her eyes she watched him dig his hand into an interior pocket of his jacket and extract a condom.

"Don't tell me," she said, laughing, "you were a Boy Scout in another life."

"In this one, actually." He smiled as he ripped open the packet and sheathed himself. "Now, where were we?"

The guttural sound that escaped her throat as he

slowly entered her body was as raw and heartfelt as the delicious sensation of him stretching and filling her. Sex had never felt so good or so right. She pushed back with her hips, meeting his every thrust, at first slow and gentle and driving her mad, then faster and faster until with a scream she gave over to her orgasm and pleasure ripped through her in ever-increasing waves. As if her climax had been his trigger, she felt him plunge even deeper and shudder against her, over and over until she lost track.

Catherine collapsed back against the tabletop, the cool wood against her shoulders a direct contrast to the perspiration-drenched heat of her body. Richard followed, and she pulled him to her, cushioning his weight with her body, wrapping her arms around him as if to let go would mean she'd float away forever.

Richard lifted his head and met her gaze.

"That was…intense," he said, still fighting to regain his breath.

"Yeah, that's one word for it," she agreed.

"I knew we'd be good together, but that? That surpassed all my expectations."

Catherine traced tiny circles on his back with a feather-light touch. She'd never felt comfortable with sex talk, especially after the act.

"Do you always conduct a postmortem after sex?" she teased.

"After making love," he corrected. "Not one for words, huh?"

"No," she admitted, letting her fingers continue tracing shapes down his spine and over the curve of his buttocks. She loved the feel of him, every glorious inch.

"Prefer action?"

"Always."

"Then I suggest we adjourn to the sofa and continue this in a little more comfort," he said, flexing his hips, causing a swell of pleasure to surge through her again in one powerful wave.

"You brought more than one condom?"

He winked at her as he straightened and slowly withdrew from her body, one hand reaching to cup her breast and caress her gently.

"As I said, I've been thinking about you a lot," he replied.

He dispensed with the used condom, wrapping it in a large cotton handkerchief before taking her hand and helping her off the table.

"So, I've had this fantasy," he started before leaning down to nip at her lips softly.

"Is that right?" she answered before giving back more of the same. "What kind of fantasy?"

He whispered into her ear, his breath sending shivers down her neck that made her skin suddenly feel more sensitive than it ever had before.

"I think we can arrange that," she answered, gently pushing his shoulders until he lay on his back on the sofa.

She extracted another packet from his pocket, then lifted one leg over his hips, straddling him and settling herself on his thighs.

"My turn," she said, her voice husky with intent.

The rain had stopped and the silence in the aftermath of the maelstrom of sensation she'd just experienced was a stark contrast to the sighs and moans, the slap of flesh, the cries of completion. A sense of time hit her with the subtlety of a cold, wet slap. It was getting late in the morning—people would be wondering where the heck she was.

She wriggled free of Richard's light clasp and grabbed her panties from the floor where she'd dropped them.

"What are you doing?"

"What does it look like I'm doing? I'm getting dressed."

"Come back here, surely we can—"

"Look—" she gestured with her hand "—this was all very nice—great, in fact—but I'm not here on holiday. I have work to do, staff to organize."

She reached over and grabbed his left arm, turning it slightly so she could read the face of his Rolex.

"And I'm running very late."

She searched around for the rest of her clothing, grimacing at the damp clinginess as she wriggled back into her riding breeches and tried to pull on her socks. Without a word, Richard rose from the sofa. In the brightening light, he looked gorgeous and she clenched her hands to prevent herself from reaching for him again.

On the table, his cell phone buzzed in its pocket. She reached over and grabbed it, catching sight of a name on the screen—Daniella—before she handed it to him.

"Maybe it's important," Catherine said as she nudged her way past him and out into the barn, desperate for some distance. While she readied their horses, she scolded herself silently.

So his ex was calling him. That wasn't so unusual, was it? Even so, she was racked with guilt. She knew she should never have given in to him. Now that she had, she only wanted him more, and he wasn't hers to have.

Richard was a city dweller. A high-flying businessman with high-flying demands on his time and his mind. Demands like the woman he was supposedly divorcing.

She didn't have time for this kind of dalliance. She wasn't that kind of girl. Of course she wasn't totally innocent, but emotionally, when it came to trust and building a relationship with someone, she was probably about as stunted as you could get. And, she told herself as she ignored the gnawing ache in the pit of her belly, she was quite happy to keep things that way. What was she even thinking allowing herself this slice of time with him?

Catherine's gut clenched tight. She knew what she'd been thinking. She'd tried to ignore the growing feelings she'd developed for him. Avoided confronting just how very much she'd looked forward to seeing him every single day. Refused to admit how much she'd craved his comfort yesterday after that awful moment in the VIP tent.

As stupid as it was, she was starting to fall for Richard Wells—fall very hard indeed—and that was the last thing she could afford to do. She couldn't love him. It was destined to fail. This interlude with Richard could never be anything more than just that, and the sooner she got her head around that the better.

But why couldn't she just take what she could for now, a little voice asked deep inside her. Compartmentalize. Wasn't that what high-flyers like Richard did in their everyday world? If she could train herself to do that, there was no reason to stop herself from enjoying him for as long as she could. And as often as she could.

Six

Richard pulled on his damp clothes with distaste. Nothing like coming back down to earth in a hurry. For a short while there, he'd thought he'd had her, had finally broken the barriers she kept so firmly between herself and the rest of the world. But then she'd gone and bolted from the tack room before he could begin to assimilate what had happened between them. Damn Daniella for choosing that moment to call him again. He'd have to see about blocking her calls.

He groaned in the silence of the tack room. He'd gone about this all wrong. He'd treated Catherine as if she were worth no more than a furtive roll in the hay, so to speak. And he knew on a gut level that she was worth so much more. Sure, the sex had been great. Better than great. But there'd been more than that. A communion of spirit. A give-and-take that he'd never felt on such a deep level before.

He should have taken her out. Wooed her slowly. Appealed to the very sensual side of her that lingered beneath the surface. Made love to her in more luxurious surroundings than those of a disused tack room, at the very least.

And yet, he couldn't regret today. Not by any definition of the word.

Out in the barn, he heard her talking to the horses. He suppressed an ironic laugh. She'd probably spoken more words to those horses today than she had to him in the whole time since they'd met. But that was going to change, he decided. And Ms. Catherine Lawson was going to let him into her life—one way or another.

Catherine still had her back to him as he approached her. He saw the exact second she sensed his presence, saw the brief stiffening of her spine, the set of her shoulders, as if she were shoring up her defenses the way she always seemed to do around him. And then, miracle of miracles, he saw her relax. He closed the short distance between them and put his arms around her waist.

She leaned back against him, and he felt a keen sense of relief. Things were going to be okay.

"I want to keep seeing you, starting tonight. Let me take you out. Dinner and dancing," he murmured against her hair, which was still loose.

"I'd like that," she answered, placing her hands over his and pressing them tightly to her.

"I'll meet you at your apartment at seven-thirty, okay?"

Catherine turned in his arms and kissed him lightly on the lips. "Are you sure you want to go out? We could stay at my place."

He knew what she was offering. In fact, every cell in

his body understood her subtext and responded in kind. But he had other plans.

"Catherine, I don't want to hide you away or make you think that this is just about sex. You're more than that."

Her blue eyes darkened and never wavered from his for what felt like a full minute. Then she slowly blinked, and a small smile curved her beautiful, lush lips.

"Thank you. That means more to me than you probably realize. Now, we'd better get going."

There was a heck of a crush in the Star Room by the time they made their way there. It was certainly the place to see people and be seen. Catherine felt as if the champagne she'd consumed at dinner was fizzing in her veins as Richard guided her through the crowd toward a slightly less frenetic spot on one side of the bar.

She was glad she'd worn high heels and a dress. She'd have felt so out of place if she'd chosen anything else. But she knew the midnight-blue satin suited her, and the way the fabric hugged her body and swayed with her every step made her feel a million times more feminine than she usually did in her customary riding breeches or jeans. Richard's expression when he'd arrived at her apartment this evening had been a testament to her hard work to transform into the kind of woman he deserved to have at his side, and he'd barely taken his eyes off her the entire time they'd dined at a nearby restaurant.

She couldn't even remember what they'd eaten, to be honest. She'd been just as rapt with his attention as he'd apparently been with hers. Now, he seemed to need constant contact with her. Tiny electric pulses ran down her arm as he gently stroked it with his hand.

"More champagne?" he asked, bending his head close to her ear.

She nodded. "I'll come with you to the bar."

"It's okay. I won't be a minute. Don't move from here or I'll never find you."

He smiled and kissed her cheek before turning and making the short distance to the bar. Catherine watched him, admiring the way he moved. Oh yes, the man could move. Another bolt of electricity hit her deep and low, making her lower muscles clench involuntarily.

"Nice to see you out socializing."

Catherine turned with a start to the source of the male voice that had come from her side. She recognized one of the visiting Argentinean team members, Alejandro Dallorso. Usually knee-deep in adoring women, he was surprisingly alone tonight.

"Nice to be out for a change."

"You work too hard." He smiled his hundred-watt smile at her.

"You play too hard," she replied with a raised eyebrow so he'd know she wasn't exactly referring to his on-field activity.

Alejandro shrugged expressively. "You're only young once, right?"

"Maybe if you played less, you'd have edged your six-goal handicap up to nine or even a ten."

The guy was loaded with talent and made playing polo look effortless, but he was definitely as interested in scoring off the field as on it.

"What? And miss all this fun? Why bother? I'm satisfied with my six, for now. It gets me what I want. Come, dance with me."

"I don't think so. Catherine is with me tonight," Richard interrupted before Catherine could respond.

Alejandro put both his hands up in mock surrender. "No problem. Maybe some other time."

Richard fought the urge to tell the other man that there would be no other time. It was ridiculous to feel so jealous, so possessive, this early—especially in a relationship that in all likelihood would end when he returned to the city. But something feral had awoken deep inside him when he'd seen the attractive Argentinean sidle up to Catherine.

He forced his lips into an approximation of a smile and nodded farewell as the man melted back into the crowd.

"Here," he said, passing a champagne flute to Catherine and clinking his against hers. "To a great night."

She smiled in response and tipped the glass up to her lips. Watching her throat move as she swallowed the sip of golden liquid sent a spear of desire straight through him. Now he'd had a taste of her, he was hungry for more. He forced his empty hand into his pocket to prevent himself from reaching out and touching her. If he did that, he'd likely lose control and want to take her from the Star Room and take her home in double quick time. He'd promised her a night out, to show her he was capable of treating her as a gentleman treated a woman.

"Richard?"

"Yeah?"

"Did you want to dance?" Catherine eyed him over the rim of her champagne glass.

He looked out over the dance floor at the bodies writhing to the beat and knew he had to be honest with her.

"No."

"Me either," she answered softly before putting a hand on his arm. "Take me to bed."

He didn't hesitate. He took her glass from her and placed it on a nearby table with his own, then took her by the hand and headed for the door. They covered the distance between the club and his guesthouse in minutes. Minutes punctuated by stolen kisses in the moonlight. By the time he thrust the door open to his suite of rooms, his heart was pounding so hard he could hear it beat inside his head.

Without even bothering to switch on the lights, he led her to his bedroom. This time he planned to take it slow.

Silver strands of moonlight strafed the wide expanse of his bed. Catherine appeared to be transfixed by the way the bed was lit, the only obvious piece of furniture in the room. Richard leaned forward to place a gentle kiss at the nape of her neck. She'd worn her hair up tonight in a casual knot high on her head that had exposed the slender line of her throat and the graceful curve of her neck. All night he'd wanted to do this.

As soon as his lips touched her skin, he was afire. His hands trembled as he placed them on her shoulders and gently eased the straps of her gown over the gentle curves. He peppered tiny kisses along the line of her shoulder, a smile curving his lips as he felt her skin tighten into tiny goose bumps and heard her breathing hitch infinitesimally. He reached for the zipper and slowly lowered it, relishing the unveiling of her beautiful back, inch by inch.

She wasn't wearing a bra, and the smooth line of her spine was unmarred as he pushed the dress away, letting the satin slide with a soft whisper all the way down her body. She wore only the tiniest of G-strings and high heels, and standing there with her back presented to him, the smooth globes of her taut buttocks bisected by only a scrap of dark fabric, he knew he'd never seen anything more beautiful.

Richard placed his hands on her shoulders again and ran them down the length of her arms before stroking back up and sliding his fingers down her spine. He felt the tremor that rippled through her as his fingers teased the outline of her panties, heard her catch and hold her breath before releasing it in a whoosh of air. He continued to trace the outline of her panties, following the line of her hips and around to her lower belly.

Touching her like this was sweet torment, but he forced himself to keep it slow. He trailed his fingertips across her flat belly and upward to the lower curve of her rib cage, following the line of each rib, one by one, until he skimmed the lower edges of her breasts. A barely suppressed groan sounded from her throat, breaking the cocoon of silence that surrounded them, and he pushed his hands higher, cupping her breasts and stroking the pads of his thumbs over her tautly budded nipples.

Catherine let her head drop back against his shoulder and pressed her buttocks back against him, against his engorged flesh. She lifted her hands to cover his, holding them tight against her, showing him what she wanted, how she needed to be touched.

Richard turned his head slightly and pressed his mouth against the exposed column of her throat, letting his teeth rasp against her skin, feeling the beat of her pulse beneath his lips, a pulse that skipped to a frantic beat. He pulled one hand from beneath hers and placed it over her own, silently encouraging her to continue to touch and stroke herself, mirroring the action with his other hand. Then, he skimmed his hand firmly down over her body, hesitating only briefly at the edge of her panties, tracing that edge across the top of her thigh and lower, until he could feel the heat of her through the dampened fabric.

He slid his hand beneath the flimsy material and let his fingers tangle briefly in her curls before dipping his middle finger in her honeyed warmth. She squirmed against him, pressing into his arousal again, forcing a groan from him that was as guttural as it was a mark of his pleasure. If she kept that up, he'd come in his pants, and he had far, far better plans for them than that.

Richard intensified his assault on her senses, sliding his moistened finger up a little, grazing her now prominent nub, at first gentle, fleeting, then with increasing pressure until he knew she was on the edge of her climax. He eased off incrementally, dragging time out, dragging the pleasure out for her. With each touch, promising her more—promising her the world.

Her entire body trembled against his as she uttered tiny, incoherent sounds, her head rolling against his shoulder, and he zoned back in on her most sensitive tissue, circling with increasing pressure until she gave herself over to the waves that now pulsed through her body. He felt all-powerful, as though he'd bestowed upon her the greatest gift, the knowledge that she, and she alone, was his entire focus. That her pleasure was paramount to him.

He scooped her into his arms and walked the short distance to the bed, laying her with exquisite care on the deliciously smooth cotton sheeting. He slipped off her high-heeled pumps, placing a kiss on the instep of each foot as he dropped her shoes to the ground, then stood and ripped his shirt over his head, unheedful of the buttons that pulled from the silk and fell to the floor. As he toed off his shoes, he undid his trousers and carefully eased them and his briefs over his straining erection, sliding them off together until he was gloriously naked.

Catherine pushed herself upright and onto her knees. She could only see Richard's silhouette in the soft, silver light streaming through his bedroom window, but she could sense him looking at her. Feel his eyes as they coasted over her body. He'd just brought her to what was probably one of the strongest climaxes she'd ever enjoyed, and yet here she was, aching for him again already. Wanting him to fill her, stretch her and become a part of her once more.

He swiftly pulled open a bedside drawer and rolled on a condom. She regretted she wouldn't have the chance to play with him a little longer, but the fact that he'd reached for protection now spoke volumes about how close he was to losing control with her altogether. The knowledge made her feel heady with power and a secret feminine awareness that she had the capacity to bring this powerful and intelligent man into such a state.

She reached out. Touching him was such a joy. He was so smooth and powerful, his muscles clearly delineated. A testament to his own personal disciplines. She lifted her face to him and he kissed her—his mouth possessive, his tongue entangling with hers in a dance more sensual than anything they could have achieved at the Star Room tonight.

She hooked her arms around his neck and dragged him closer, fusing their skin together. She felt his fingers loosen the few pins that held her hair up until it slid in its mass down her back.

The warmth of his hands followed the path of her hair, and tiny trickles of electricity passed through her skin. She'd never felt such an awareness of any man before, never wanted to be as much a part of him as he was rapidly becoming a part of her. Self-preservation, reason, distance—all three fled from her consciousness as they lay down on the bed together, as his body covered hers. And when he entwined his fingers with hers, lifting her arms up over her head to rest on the voluminous feather pillows, and slid his hard flesh slowly inside her, she knew that no matter how hard she tried, a piece of her heart would always belong to Richard Wells.

Seven

It was her day off. She was surprised the sheikh had insisted so vehemently on her taking the time, especially with it being a tournament day. Realistically, given that the day was supposedly her own, she should be down at the beach—catching a few waves, relaxing in the sun—instead of sipping champagne and balancing on high heels on the grassy field. But she'd discovered over the past two weeks that it was anatomically impossible for her to be away from Richard. The ache that lived inside her was monumental. He consumed every waking thought and a huge percentage of her sleeping ones, too.

When he'd insisted she accompany him to the VIP tents today and enjoy the polo purely as a spectator, she'd demurred. As much as she wanted to be with him, she also recognized that from time to time she had to create the illusion of independence. At least make him think that, for some of the time, she wasn't living minute by minute until they could be together again.

The past few days had been intense as they'd given in to their powerful attraction to one another to the exclusion of all others and any other activity. While her days had been busy with the horses and her usual duties, her nights had been full of the wonder of learning every amazing inch of Richard's body. And in their quiet times together—over a picnic in his bed, a shared dinner at her apartment, or even just a drive around Suffolk County—she learned a little more about what made Richard Wells tick.

When she'd tried to raise objections to accompanying him today, he'd simply brushed them aside. When she brought up the issue of her boss, he'd told her he'd already discussed her being there as his companion and had received no objections.

Companion. It was such an innocuous word and could mean so much—or so little.

She knew he was only in the Hamptons for a month and yes, realistically, she could expect to see a bit more of him even after he'd returned to the city, especially for the finals of the Clearwater Media Cup. Deep down, though, she knew her allure would fade and that he'd eventually find activities closer to home that would keep him in the city. It hurt but, she told herself over and over, it was worth it to have had this incredible time with him.

Catherine looked at the spectators who mingled and drank and brushed against one another. The tent seethed with people from all walks of life, but there was one thing they all had in common—money—and that was something Catherine would never be able to compete with. So, she'd have fun while she was here with Richard, and then somehow she'd find the strength to say goodbye when it was time for this idyll to end.

Her eye was suddenly caught by an older gentleman making a beeline toward her. There was something familiar about him that she couldn't quite put her finger on.

"A beautiful woman like yourself should never be left alone." The man smiled warmly.

Despite herself, Catherine smiled in return. As a pickup line it left a lot to be desired, but she had the feeling his interest in her wasn't sexual, which was a relief. Within the heady and glamorous world of polo, it wasn't unusual for liaisons to be formed and unformed between people who were virtual strangers.

"How could anyone be alone in a crush like this?" she answered, taking a sip of her champagne.

"You'd be surprised how lonely a person can be in company," the man replied. "I detect a bit of an accent there. Australian?"

"No, I'm a New Zealander. Although it's been a long time since I was home."

"Hmm," he nodded. "Trouble at home?"

"Not my trouble, but I still wanted to remove myself from it. Besides, working with horses is all I've ever really wanted to do. I would have been foolish not to have taken the opportunity to work with the sheikh and his horses when it presented itself."

"It always pays to follow your dream," he said sagely. "Although it can come at a great personal cost at times."

Through the throng, Catherine saw Richard making his way toward her, his dark brows drawn in a straight line. Surely he wasn't jealous, she thought. He had no right to be. After she'd seen and heard his proprietary manner at the Star Room that night, she realized he didn't want to share her with anyone, but seriously, to be annoyed with her for talking to an older man? It was ridiculous.

"Catherine." Richard nodded in her direction. "Is everything all right?"

"And why shouldn't it be?" the older man beside her said, his tone challenging.

Richard didn't take his eyes off her. "Is this man bothering you?"

"No, of course not," she sputtered. What the heck was going on?

"Come on, then, let's find our places in the stands."

Without so much as acknowledging the man who'd been talking to her, Richard took her arm and guided her toward the stands. Irritation rose within her. Perhaps it was time they established some ground rules. Starting with him not dictating who she talked to.

"I don't think I want to be with you right now," she finally managed through her anger and yanked her arm free of his hold.

"Trust me. You didn't want to talk to him anyway."

"How would I know? I never really got the opportunity. And while I'm on the subject, who appointed you my keeper? You have no right to say who I can and can't speak to."

Catherine bent down, slipped off her high heels and began to walk toward the road that led to the grooms' apartments.

"Catherine! Stop, please."

Richard's voice came from close behind her, encouraging her to step up her pace. The warmth of his fingers soon closed over her shoulders. She should have known he'd follow.

"Leave me alone. I'm too angry to talk to you right now."

"I'm sorry. I was wrong. I shouldn't have behaved like that."

Catherine stopped in her tracks. An apology. She hadn't expected that. Men like him didn't make a habit of saying they were sorry. At least not in her experience.

"Apology accepted," she said grudgingly. "But I'm still mad."

"Look, why don't I take you for an early dinner to explain. We'll get away from here for a bit."

She looked at him closely.

"Sure," she said, sliding her feet back into her shoes. "Promise me one thing, though."

"What's that?"

"That you won't piss me off again until after I've eaten."

His laughter warmed her heart. She really didn't want any conflict between them—not during the short time they'd have together. She allowed him to tug her close, accepted the pressure of his lips against hers and answered back with a passion that would leave him in no doubt of her forgiveness.

They headed out in Richard's car—some top-of-the-line thing, judging by the plush leather upholstery and the dashboard that looked as though it wouldn't be amiss on a fighter plane.

"Where are we going?" she asked as they drove along Millstone Road.

"Noyack Bay. There's a good seafood place there. You do like seafood, don't you?"

"Love it," she reassured him.

He wasn't kidding when he said the place was good. It

was better than good. The food was delicious, the decor luxurious and comfortable, and the company—well, the company was one hundred percent focused on ensuring she had a great time. Given his attentive behavior right now, if Catherine hadn't seen the way he'd snubbed that other man back at the polo grounds, she'd never have thought him capable of such a thing.

The contrast was a little disconcerting, and as much as she hated to burst the intimate bubble of attention she was receiving she had to know why he'd been so incredibly impolite. Catherine leaned back in the deep cushioned rattan chair and looked out over the Bay. She took a deep breath before looking back at Richard.

"Tell me, why were you so rude to that man back at the tent? You acted like—"

"Like I couldn't stand the sight of him?" Richard interrupted drily.

"Well, yeah. He was only chatting to me. So what's the story? Why did you behave like that?"

"He's my father."

The glass in her hand slid from her fingers, falling to the tiled floor with a resounding smash and shattering glass around the tables and chairs. Like a well-oiled machine, staff materialized from nowhere, sweeping away the debris, mopping up the champagne she'd been drinking and bringing a fresh glass filled with the delicious French vintage Richard had ordered for her with her dinner.

She knew she'd never drink it. Not now. Not with the shock of Richard's revelation still reverberating through her body with an echoing chill. *His father!* And he treated him like that?

The cold shock was rapidly followed by an ache in her chest. She'd give anything to be able to speak to her father again—to feel his big, strong arms around her one more time, to ask his advice on a difficult pony. Anything.

"But why?" Her voice came out in croak. "What happened to make you so angry at him?"

She knew he'd been angry. She had seen firsthand the blaze of fury that shone from Richard's gray eyes, turning them to steel. But worse, she'd seen faint hope in his father's eyes and then seen that hope dashed as effectively as the crystal champagne flute she'd just dropped to the floor.

Her shock must have shown on her face. Richard's eyes narrowed, and he reached across the table to hold her hand.

"You'd have to understand what happened to understand why."

"So tell me. What on earth was so bad that you can't even be civil to him anymore?"

That Richard was the angry one was clear to her now as she replayed the short scene back in her head. His father had spoken directly to him. It was Richard who'd acted as if he didn't exist, hadn't so much as spoken. It was Richard who'd cut him out of her sphere and led her away.

"It's complicated," he hedged.

"We have time. I'm listening," she encouraged.

Richard sighed and leaned back in his chair, looking at her across the table as if he were weighing what he had to say. Catherine found herself holding her breath. The man in front of her was nothing like the passionate and generous lover she'd spent her nights with this past week. Nothing like the playful, teasing suitor who'd shadowed her until she'd finally agreed to a date with him. No, this was the corporate Richard. The man she didn't know. The man who was as far removed from her as the earth from the sun. And she knew—by getting this close, by probing into something so deep and so personal—she risked getting badly burned.

"You have to understand a bit about my father before we go any further." Richard sighed and gestured to the waiter. "Coffee, please, and keep it coming. We may be a while."

Catherine waited patiently for the waiter to return with their coffee and smiled her thanks as he added milk and the two sugars that were her only sweet vice. Once he'd gone again, she lifted her cup to her lips, watching Richard carefully over the rim as she sipped.

"My father's family came over from Ireland. My great-grandfather was a typesetter by trade but was suspected of printing and distributing seditious material. I understand the family got out of the country and onto a boat so fast that they didn't have time to pack more than a few sets of clothes and loaves of bread. When they arrived here they had next to nothing, and he didn't find it easy to find work right away.

"Over time, though, he got back into printing and eventually had his own small press. When my grandfather took it over, he turned it into a series of papers being distributed not just citywide but statewide. By the time my father joined the family business, it had expanded even farther. Their interests are now global."

"That's quite an achievement over just three generations," Catherine commented.

Richard nodded in agreement. "Pretty phenomenal, especially when you know how many other businesses thrived then failed due to economic crises, wars, even something as simple as poor circulation."

"So why didn't you follow in your father's footsteps?" It was clear to her that that was the crux of the problem.

"Why? Because he's a stubborn old coot who wouldn't listen to new ideas for expansion or growth. I was nearly done with my degree when we started talking about my future with the family firm. I had ideas I couldn't wait to implement. It was way past time we hopped on the digital express that was pulling out of the station, but he wouldn't listen to me. Said I lacked the experience to pull off the expansion I wanted to head. Said I'd have to prove my worth and bide my time before developing my ideas any further.

"I told him he could stick his job, that he was entrenched in the dark ages. I'd grown up with ink running through my veins, had spent every holiday working with him or in different departments of the business. I knew what was involved, I knew what was at stake and I knew that if I didn't act soon for him, Wells & Son would eventually hit the wall."

And has it? The question echoed silently in her head. She could understand Richard's frustration, but by the same token, she could see his father's point of view. Sure, Richard had had some experience in the industry—probably more than most other interns—but she could imagine that his enthusiasm for change had to be tempered with the experience of living and working the industry for years.

She carefully put her cup down on its saucer and leaned forward, resting her elbows on the table, propping her chin in her hands.

"How did he take it? You telling him to stick his job."

Richard shook his head slowly before answering. "I

have to hand it to the old man. He's got balls. He actually laughed at me. Told me the door was always open but that I needed to grow up some more before I could work for him. He actually let me go."

"So what did you do next?"

"Finished my degree. Graduated summa cum laude. Set up Clearwater Media with Seb and showed my father how it was supposed to be done."

"And you haven't spoken to him since?"

"No."

"You must miss him."

"Hey, it's water under the bridge now. I've made my own future from the ground up. Clearwater has turned into one of the fastest-growing media companies worldwide. It has solid foundations, and we still have a long way to go. We will be around for generations."

It struck Catherine that Richard's future generations would never get to know his father if the men didn't mend their differences. She gathered up her courage to ask out loud the question she'd silently posed.

"Has your father's firm gone to the wall like you said?"

Richard's laugh lacked any humor. "No, of course not. The old man was far too canny for that. Seems he'd been intending to expand digitally for years but was handpicking his team to implement it. Clearly he never considered me good enough for that."

The hurt in that statement cut to Catherine's heart. The two men must have been very close. To have severed all ties must have been immeasurably painful to them both for different reasons. And both were obviously too proud to reach out and rebuild.

She didn't condone what Richard had done. Not by any means. He must have come across as brash and arrogant to his more experienced father. She'd seen it so often herself with younger grooms pitting their limited skills against those with a lifetime of experience working with horses. But his father hadn't done the right thing by Richard either. No wonder he'd strived so hard to succeed. And no wonder he took so many opportunities to laud his success in the news. She supposed, under normal circumstances, that she would have been unlikely to have heard as much about Richard Wells if he hadn't been so hell-bent on shoving his prowess in his father's face.

His hurt, his determination and drive, even his upbringing—all of those things combined to make Richard who he was today. And as much as she failed to fit into his world, she couldn't help but love the man in it.

"So, there you have it. What would you like to do for the rest of the evening?" Richard broke into her thoughts.

That was it? Subject now closed? Judging by the look on his face, the topic was most definitely no longer open to further discussion. But a part of her burned to help Richard make things right with his father—before it was too late for both of them.

Eight

Richard lay back against the pillows, his heart still thudding in his chest, thunderbolts of pleasure still pounding through his body. It didn't matter how they made love, how fast or how often, the result was always the same as the first time. An unending sense of completion—of rightness. He so wasn't ready for this. The ink on the papers to his divorce from Daniella was barely dry and here he was, imagining that Catherine was "the one"?

Man, if his friends knew what he was thinking, they'd call him certifiable. But there were no other words for how he felt—for how Catherine made him feel.

She lay sprawled over his body, her legs entangled with his, her hair a curtain across his chest, her head just over his heart. Did she know that it beat for her? Did she understand that she was becoming more and more important to him with every day that passed? Even though he wasn't ready for anything permanent—maybe never would be again—he couldn't deny that she brought out the best in him and he liked that. He'd forgotten what the best was.

In return, he wanted to be that man who brought the smile to her face, the quiet humor to her eyes, the cries of pleasure to her lips. She hadn't looked so happy today, though. There'd been a reserve in her eyes that had appeared when he'd caught his father talking to her in the VIP tent and, despite his explanation for their estrangement, that reserve had remained. It wasn't until they'd come back to his place after stopping at the beach to walk along the white sand and watch the waves roll in off the Atlantic that she'd lost that slightly haunted look in her eyes.

Richard let his fingers draw lazy shapes over Catherine's back, relishing the softness of her skin, the hidden strength in her long, lean form. She'd said nothing about him and his dad not being on speaking terms. Aside from her original anger at his behavior, there hadn't been so much as a hint of disapproval.

Playing their conversation over in his head, he started to feel uncomfortable, wondering how she'd really felt hearing about the rift for the first time. The person he'd been, the man he'd described to her, had been very young and hotheaded—totally passionate about his cause, as he saw it. His anger toward his father had driven him to succeed, to refuse to accept failure as an option. He supposed he should thank the old man for that, if nothing else.

Suddenly his churlishness left a bitter taste in his mouth. His father had never actually held him back or cut ties. That had been Richard's choice. There were hundreds of things his father could have done—financially and socially—to completely shut him down if he had really wanted to retaliate, but he'd done none of them. He'd let his only son make his own path.

Looking back now, Richard seriously doubted he would consider hiring someone so young and inexperienced to implement a major policy change within Clearwater Media. Sebastian would have him declared insane, and invoke the power of attorney they each held for one another in extenuating circumstances, if he were ever so foolish as to entertain the idea. As much as it galled him to admit it, his father had been right to do what he did. To step away. To let him sink or swim.

The distance that had grown between them over the issue had been more Richard's doing than his dad's, but how could he even begin to rectify the issue after so many years, and so much anger and bitterness? They were equally pigheaded and stubborn. It had sadly become easier to be apart than to try and mend the gaping hole in what had once been a strong bond between them.

Catherine stirred from her languor and lifted her head, distracting him from his thoughts.

"You okay?" she asked.

"Yeah, just doing some thinking."

"Oh? Good things, I hope."

"Good and bad."

She shifted and nestled into his side, snuggling up against him and drifting her hand across his chest. He loved her touch. It did the most incredible things to him. For now, though, he was happy to simply lie here.

"Want to talk about it?"

"No, I'm okay. Besides, I'd rather talk about you.

We've spent all this time together and you've hardly told me anything about yourself."

"There's not much to know."

"Try me. Start with what you want."

"That's simple. You."

She pressed a kiss against his skin and followed it up with a tiny nip that sent a spear of longing straight to his groin.

"Aside from me—" he laughed "—what do you want long-term? What's the big picture for Ms. Catherine Lawson?"

"Ah, that's easy. I want my own stables. Initially to teach those who can afford it, but one day I'd like to be able to teach kids who have it tough—whether financially or emotionally—to learn to ride and care for horses. It's what I've always wanted to do. There are so many kids out there desperate for something to do, for someone to spend time with them, for the chance to love something. So, yeah. That's the long-term plan. How I'm going to get there—" she shrugged "—is the hard part."

"Why not start with finding sponsorship? Your idea is bound to resonate with enough of the money men needing an outlet for charitable funds or positive publicity associated with community projects. Then you'd have your start-up costs taken care of, and you wouldn't have to wait to expand the second stage of your dream."

She shook her head. "It's not that easy."

"Why not? Have you tried?"

"No," she hedged.

"What's stopping you?"

"You wouldn't understand."

"Try me," he encouraged her gently. "You might be surprised. I have contacts, you know."

"You remember what happened last week, when those women said those things?"

"Yes," he said. "Something to do with your dad, right?"

"Yeah," she sighed. "He worked with horses on the polo circuit, too. He was a good player, but he lacked the competitive spirit to ever go up the ranks. But he was damn good at making polo ponies."

"Like you."

"I'm not even half as good as he was."

"If you really only have half his talent, he must have been quite a man."

Richard rubbed his hand down Catherine's back and pulled her in closer.

"He was. His reputation was huge no matter where we went, and he was the center of my universe. Mum was always quite happy being on the social edges of polo. She loved the hype of being Del Lawson's wife."

Catherine fell quiet for a moment, and Richard waited patiently for her to continue. From the tension he could feel in her body, he knew what was coming wouldn't be pleasant, and he sensed it was already exacting a toll from her.

"I was about fifteen when it happened. A patron had seen the ponies Dad had worked with during a tournament at Palm Beach. He approached Dad with an offer to work with a low-goal team and a string of ponies through the New Zealand season with a view to putting them in tournaments in the U.K. later on.

"He was so excited. The chance of working with a talented group of international riders, bringing them up to a higher level of play and improving their ponies, was more than he could resist. Of course it wasn't as good as it seemed. Nothing ever is."

"The guy was rigging the team?"

"He was doping the horses. He had brought with him a vet who gave the ponies doctored supplements. Something went wrong with the cocktail he was giving them. Dad had no idea—he'd believed it was the usual supplement, one commonly used pretty much everywhere. The ponies went on the field for a tournament and things started going wrong. The officials ordered an investigation."

"Going wrong?"

"One of the horses collapsed and died on the field. The others began showing signs of extreme distress. Dad did what he could, but it was too late. Of course the fingers all started pointing at him. He could never prove that he'd had nothing to do with the incident, and it destroyed his reputation. No one would hire him."

"Did he fight back? Didn't your polo association order an investigation?"

"Yes, but Dad was head groom. He and he alone had the final say on how the ponies were fed, supplemented and trained. No one believed he'd had no idea about what the vet had been doing—or that the patron was complicit. Dad took the rap and eventually it killed him."

Richard felt hot tears begin to fall upon his chest. He was filled with a helplessness that was foreign to him. He wanted to make everything right in Catherine's world, but he knew he could no more turn back the clock and fix the problem than he could spin glass from moonbeams.

"Mum was horrified. Her world, as she knew it, was destroyed. She distanced herself from him as soon as she could and ended up going to Australia and finding herself a new partner before she and Dad were even divorced. I stayed with Dad. I couldn't leave him. He had nothing else. He'd worshipped Mum. When she left, it was as if she believed he'd been capable of doing those things he'd been accused of. That hurt him more than anything.

"He started drinking—heavily. He got a job when I was sixteen, breaking horses on a farm where his reputation hadn't quite caught up with him. But then one day a buyer recognized him and brought it to his boss's attention. No one looked at him the same after that, and one night, after a few drinks, he took one of the horses and rode out into the bush. The horse came back, but it was two days before rescue workers found Dad. The coroner's report said he'd died of exposure and the rumors said suicide. But I know he died of a broken heart."

"And you're saying what happened in the tent the other day, that's what you have to deal with? People talking about your father's reputation?"

"Who on earth would sponsor the child of the man who created world headlines with what happened? It's been twelve years, but memories are long—you saw that. When I was younger, all I wanted to do was to clear Dad's name. But the more years that pass, the more I realize how impossible that is."

Richard swallowed back the anger that welled within him and forced himself to speak calmly.

"Clearly Sheikh Adham didn't feel that way or you wouldn't be working for him."

"No. I was very lucky there. Soon after Dad died, I was helping out at the grounds in Clevedon, and he was there. One of his horses got spooked by a stray dog that wandered onto the field. I caught her and calmed her down before she could hurt herself. He offered me a job, so, with nothing left for me in New Zealand, I took it."

"What happened to the guy who let your dad take the fall for him?"

"He's around. Not in the league the sheikh competes in, so it's some comfort I haven't bumped into him yet."

"And is he still up to the same tricks?"

"I don't know."

"I bet it wouldn't be too hard to find out."

Catherine sighed. "Probably not, but that's not my fight anymore. If I thought I could, I'd move heaven and earth to clear my dad's name—for his sake, not for mine. I reconciled myself a couple years ago to the fact that that kind of thing is totally out of my reach. The only thing I can do now is keep doing what I do, as well as I can do it. The sheikh's a generous employer. I'm paid very well. I already have a deposit saved for a small farm. In time I'll have the balance of what I need to be able to set up, and once I've proved myself—hopefully before I'm too old to get up on a horse—" she laughed quietly "—then I'll have my own reputation to stand on when I start applying for loans for the rest. As for sponsorship—that's still just a dream."

Catherine started drawing little circles on his belly, her light touch making his skin tingle and sending more demanding sensations through his body. But her next words dashed his ardor more effectively than a bucket of ice water.

"I'd do anything to have my dad back, Richard. I know you've had your differences with yours, but you only get one father in your life. You and your father used to be close—I could hear that in your voice even as you told me how the two of you fell out. You miss that closeness. You miss him. Don't waste any more time, because when he's gone you will never have that opportunity to make things right again. Never."

Richard's instinctive reaction to his father, to her words, rushed through him. Miss his dad? She had to be kidding. But as much as he didn't want to acknowledge that truth, he knew she was right.

After walking her home, Richard thought long and hard about what she'd said. Especially, what she'd told him about her father and how intensely loyal she remained to his memory weighed on his mind. He was surprised to feel a pang of envy that she had a far stronger relationship with her dead father than he had with his father who was still living.

She'd opened his eyes earlier in the evening to how idiotic his behavior appeared to anyone not aware of the situation that had led to the rift between father and son. At the time, though, it had been so real—the hurt, the distrust, the lack of confidence. It occurred to him now that he wouldn't have worked under his father's umbrella forever. It had been an introduction to the industry he loved, but he'd have wanted to branch out, to pursue his own ambitions.

Richard thrived on the cut and thrust of taking something new and expanding it to its fullest potential. Developing ideas with Seb had given them a powerful edge over their competition. The way they worked was tailor-made to his intensity.

If anything, his father had probably done him a favor by not agreeing to his demands. He shoved a hand through his hair and leaned against one of the moonlit fence railings. Why did life have to be so damn complicated?

Here was Catherine, who would probably give anything to have five more minutes with her father, and Seb, whose father was battling cancer, the threat of losing that battle hanging like Damocles's sword over his best friend's head every day. And then there was him. Letting pride and an unhealthy dose of ego stand in the way of reaching out to the only father he'd ever have.

Richard pushed off the railings with a muttered curse and stalked back to the guesthouse. There were no easy answers anymore, but he was certain of one thing. Whatever had passed between him and his father had well and truly passed. He was his own man now, and part of being that man was owning up to his mistakes.

He'd been happy to take everything his father had ever given him, but he'd done nothing in return. The thought of losing him, without ever having made the time to mend the prideful fences between them, sliced through him like a knife.

With each step he took back to the house, he firmed his resolve that he would not let that happen. He would talk to his father at the game this coming weekend, starting with an apology and hopefully ending with a new basis for them to move forward.

His eyes had been opened. And he had Catherine to thank for that.

Nine

It had been a busy week. The struggle to balance the demands of her job and her nights with Richard had hit Catherine full force this morning, leaving her feeling out of sorts when she awoke.

There was a match later today, and she busied herself with her usual chores, making time pass quickly. By the time the ponies were prepared, she was about ready to fall into bed. That was a faint hope, she conceded grimly, with a game due to start at four o'clock. She looked around at the field, anxious for the sight of Richard.

Things had been different between them this week. *He'd* been different. She'd seen his ex-wife's name on his caller ID several times, and despite his attentions to Catherine, the other woman's constant contact with Richard made her feel unsettled. On top of that was her concern that maybe she'd overstepped the mark when she'd urged Richard to make up with his father. It really wasn't her place to have said anything, but in the face of what she'd learned about their estrangement, she couldn't stop herself.

In the distance, a dark head caught her attention, and her heart did that strange flip-flop it always did whenever she saw him. She waved but Richard, despite looking straight in her direction, didn't appear to notice her. Or if he did, he was avoiding her. Catherine tried not to feel hurt but she knew she was in too deep for the snub, real or imagined, not to sting a little. If he wasn't on the lookout for her, it clearly spelled out something else—he was definitely cooling things off.

Would it be better to make a clean break and be done with it? She knew he only had a few more days before he had to go back to the city. Instantly, her heart rebelled. No, she was in this for however long she could take it—and for however much of him she could have. The memories would give her something to cling to as she refocused on her dream. Maybe it was even time to have a chat with a bank manager and see just how much she could borrow to start things moving with her riding school. She had a strong feeling that she would need to be very busy to keep her mind off Richard Wells, and what he'd come to mean to her, once he left.

Her eyes tracked Richard's every move. He was looking for someone—someone who wasn't her, that much was obvious. When she saw him stiffen, she knew he'd found who he was looking for. She watched as he strode purposefully toward a group and singled someone out, drawing him away from the throng of spectators.

His father! Richard was talking to his father. Catherine's hand flew to her mouth, and her weariness was forgotten as she watched the two men face one another.

She was too far away to catch the expression on the older man's face, but she saw him reach out to clasp his son's hand in his, and then Richard drew his father close, closing the older man in an embrace that brought tears to her eyes.

The two men stayed that way for some time, and Catherine forced herself to look away before she became a blubbering mess. Richard had taken the first monumental step. Slowly it began to sink in that what she'd said to him last week had actually meant something to him.

No wonder he'd been quiet. She'd learned from watching him that he was single-minded in his purpose—his pursuit of her was a prime example. He'd been weighing up what she'd said, how he felt and whether he was prepared to do something about it.

She dashed away the tears from her cheeks and turned back to the pony lines. He'd done the right thing. Her step was a great deal lighter as she rejoined her grooms and double-checked the ponies and players were all ready to go for the first chukka that was due to start shortly.

It wasn't until the stomping of the divots at halftime that she caught sight of him again. He was still with his father, their heads close together as they spoke, not even looking at the field. Again, she felt that flutter deep in her chest. She had it bad, she admitted to herself. Real bad.

A couple of the local girls she'd taken on for the season came up and stood alongside Catherine by the railings.

"That's Richard Wells, isn't it?" said one to the other.

"Yeah, I heard he was back on the market. It's a shame he's too old for us. I wonder if he could be persuaded to look at a younger model next time around," the other said and laughed. "He's totally hot and filthy rich."

"He's not on the market, from what I've heard around the tents."

Catherine's ears pricked up. While they hadn't deliberately kept their time together a big secret, they hadn't exactly showcased their relationship in the public eye, either. Were the two girls talking about her without even realizing it?

"What? He's got someone new?"

"No, I heard he's still married and that there's a reunion on the cards."

The contents of Catherine's stomach solidified and shifted sharply, lodging at the base of her throat. An icy chill drenched her body from head to foot.

He was still married?

Murmuring something about checking equipment, she stumbled away. No wonder he'd had so many calls from his ex. Catherine felt as if she were being torn apart in every way. She loved him but he was forever forbidden to her. She didn't do married men. It was one of her absolute irrevocable rules about life. She'd seen how it had destroyed her father when her mother had drifted away from him and started a new relationship before they'd even divorced. Catherine had sworn she would never be party to anything like that in her life.

She was such a fool. She should have known, should have followed her instincts and stayed away from him. Should have stayed out of his arms and out of his bed. Should never—ever—have fallen in love with him.

Catherine threw herself into work for the rest of the afternoon, and when Richard texted her later that evening, she put him off, telling him she was extremely tired and wanted nothing more than a soak in a hot bath and an early night. When he easily accepted her excuse, she didn't know whether to be pleased or disappointed. Was he relieved that she wasn't available tonight? Did it mean he was already preparing to let her go?

She reminded herself that she'd gone into their relationship with her eyes wide open. That she'd known there could never be a future for them together because their worlds were so far apart that she could never dream of bridging the gap. She deserved this sense of loss—it was punishment for daring to reach out and take what was not hers to own. But knowing all that didn't make any of it any easier.

Richard threw his cell phone on his bed in frustration. Something was wrong. This was the fourth day in a row that Catherine had refused to see him, and he still had no logical reason why. He missed her with an ache that drew from the soles of his feet all the way up through his body—an ache he was desperate to relieve. He hadn't wanted to admit just how much she'd gotten under his skin, how important she'd become to him. This was supposed to have been a fling, a summer affair to get him back in the single man's swing of things, but it was turning out to be so very much more.

The distance in her tone the past few days puzzled him. Friendly yet remote. And while she'd sounded happy for him when he'd told her about how he and his father had agreed to put the past behind them, that had been it. There'd been no further enquiries, no gentle encouragement. None of what he'd come to expect in her company. The loss of her companionship struck him harder than he could have imagined.

He tried to rationalize it. Maybe she'd decided to back off a bit and let him spend time with his father while he was in the Hamptons, but even that rang empty as an excuse. There was no reason why she couldn't still be a part of it. He'd hoped she might have wanted to share his joy, to talk it over with him because it wasn't going to be an easy relationship to rebuild. He and his father were too similar on many levels—but they were both committed to making it work this time.

Richard paced his bedroom floor. It was as if Catherine had reverted back to how she'd been the day he first saw her. Reserved and aloof. Rejecting him. Something had happened to make her withdraw like this; he just knew it. But what?

His phone buzzed from among the expensive bed linens, and he snatched it up. Maybe she'd changed her mind. The number on the caller ID taunted him for his hopes. Sebastian.

"Yeah, Seb, how are you?"

"Haven't seen much of you this vacation, my friend, what with the club and keeping that sister of mine in line. Everything okay?"

"I've been—" he hesitated a moment before continuing "—preoccupied. But I'm free tonight. How about we meet for a drink?"

Later that evening, the two men reclined in plush seats in Sebastian's den at the main house, comfortable in one another's company.

"So, did you take my advice?" Sebastian asked, taking a sip of his drink.

"To get laid?" Richard snorted a laugh. "That would be telling, and a gentleman never tells."

Sebastian smiled in return and raised his glass in a toast. "Good for you. Has it helped?"

Had it helped, Richard wondered? Sure, it had taken his mind off his divorce from Daniella, but *helped?* He twirled his brandy in his glass, seemingly absorbed by the amber liquid, but his mind was focused very much on just one person, Catherine. On how she looked astride a horse, so in command, so lithe and strong. How she looked first thing in the morning, her long hair tousled and spread across his pillow. The expression in her eyes as he entered her body, giving herself to him with utter abandon.

Every muscle in his body tautened, and his fingers clenched against the tumbler holding his drink.

"Richard?" Sebastian prompted.

"I believe I've fallen in love."

Saying the words out loud sent a shudder of fear through him. How could he be saying it or even be thinking it? He'd just come out of a nasty, bitter divorce—the by-product of a marriage entered into in haste, with a partner with whom he'd had little in common.

"Are you sure about this?" Seb looked at him seriously across the coffee table.

"Yeah, I know. I've taken this route before. But this is different, you know? *She's* different."

"Does she feel the same way about you?"

"I don't know. Right now she's avoiding me."

"A ploy, maybe?"

Both men knew all too well how Daniella had behaved. How she'd sulk like a child one minute and then vamp herself up the next.

"No. I'm sure of that. Catherine wouldn't be bothered with that kind of thing. She's not into games."

"Catherine? You mean the sheikh's head groom?"

Richard nodded.

"Wow, she's different from Daniella, all right. In fact, I'd say she's her polar opposite."

"I know. I thought it would just be some mutual fun, you know? But she's come to mean so much more. She's even got me talking to my dad again."

"Hey, Richard, that's great. She must be pretty amazing to get you to cross that bridge. I mean, I know Daniella wanted you and your dad to reconcile, but that was more from the point of view of what you'd stand to inherit than anything else."

"I know. And yeah, Catherine is amazing. She made me see things—*me,* more precisely—from a different perspective."

"Well," Sebastian said, getting up to refresh their drinks, "that kills the rumors flying around the tents at the moment."

"Rumors?"

"Yeah, that your divorce isn't final and that a reconciliation is in the works."

Richard laughed out loud. "Where the hell did that come from?"

Sebastian shrugged. "You know how these things start. Someone gets the wrong end of the stick, and before you know it, it's gospel."

Richard accepted his refill from Sebastian and considered his best friend's words. Was it possible that Catherine had heard those rumors and, rather than asking him if they were true, had believed them? Choosing to withdraw rather than confront? That would be her style, especially given her history.

"Just when did these rumors start? Do you know?" he asked.

"Couple of days ago. Vanessa asked me if it was

true and offered to pay to get your head examined if it was."

The timing made sense. If Catherine *had* heard the rumor about him and Daniella, then she'd definitely have withdrawn from their relationship. She was old-fashioned like that—her sense of right and wrong was as indelibly marked on her as her fingerprints. In some ways, her old-fashioned demeanor was at odds with the lifestyle the polo set was famed for, but he'd found it both refreshing and challenging. No less challenging now would be convincing her that what she might have overheard was completely and utterly wrong. There was only one woman he wanted in his life—he knew that now with complete and utter certainty. And that woman was Catherine Lawson.

Ten

Catherine was bone weary—pretty much "situation normal" these days, she thought ironically. Her feet dragged on the stairs that led to her second-floor apartment in the groom's quarters. It had been a difficult day all around. One of the sheikh's favorite horses had come up lame and he wasn't happy, and to cap things off, a couple of the female grooms had gotten into a snit over some British player and she'd had to intervene before the girls did some serious damage to each other.

The prospect of falling into bed and managing to sleep until the morning was strongly alluring right now. The reality, she knew, would be something different. Since she'd made the decision not to see Richard again, she'd felt heartsick. No matter how hard she pushed herself, she couldn't get him out of her mind. Nor could she ignore the deep sense of loss at her decision.

She'd endured worse, she told herself, and she'd

survived. She'd known Richard, what, nearly a month? It was ridiculous to think she had fallen in love with him so completely. Simply and utterly ridiculous.

A shadow stepped out from the alcove by her front door, and her heart leaped in her chest when she recognized Richard's tall frame. In the dim light offered by the overhead lamp, he looked mighty fine to her eyes.

"We need to talk," he said, his voice deep and pitched low.

"Sure," she said, summoning every ounce of false bravado in her arsenal.

She could do this. She could let him go. Obviously that was why he was here—to tell her the truth about him and his wife. To say "Thanks for the memories, but I'm getting on with my life now." Her hand shook as she tried to put her key into the lock. Richard's hand closed over hers, taking the key.

"Here, let me. You look exhausted." He opened the door and ushered her in before him. "Tough day?"

Tough life, she answered silently but gave a short nod as she eased her boots off and headed to the kitchen.

"Coffee? Sorry, I can't offer you anything alcoholic," she said stiffly.

After observing firsthand her father's slide into the bottle, she reserved her drinking for social occasions only.

"No, I'm okay, thanks."

"Do you want to sit down?" she asked, keen to get off her feet herself, but more than that, she wanted him to be still and in one place. Right now she felt as if he were looming over her.

"No. I won't."

Despite all her pep talks to herself about ending their relationship, the knowledge that he didn't plan to be here long sent her heart plummeting to the soles of her feet. He had to be here to say goodbye. She wished to heck he'd just say it and get it over with—so she could start kidding herself that she was getting over him.

"Why haven't you seen me?"

His question startled her. She'd thought he'd have been glad of being given the distance—at least that way there'd be no messy goodbyes. He could have done this with a phone call.

"I've been busy and so have you. How are things going with your father? I thought I saw you together again the other day."

"Nice parry, Catherine, but you won't distract me. Tell me the truth." He stepped closer, took both her hands in his and locked gazes with her. "You owe me that much at least."

"I…I'm not into goodbyes. I just thought it would be easier, that's all."

"Easier? Goodbyes? What makes you think I want to say goodbye to you?"

"Well, it's coming up to the end of your vacation. You'll be leaving. Going back to work, your other life."

Your wife.

"And you think I don't want to see you anymore? That I can just walk away from you like that?"

His fingers curled around hers, tight, making it impossible to pull away.

"Look, I knew the score right from the start. It was only supposed to be a fling, and it has been. A great one. But we both knew all along it had to end."

"It doesn't have to end, Catherine," he said, his voice calm and deep.

Shock tore through her. He wanted to keep their affair

going even while he was considering reuniting with his wife?

"Yes, it does." She shook her head and yanked free of his hold, wrapping her arms around herself to stop him from taking her hands again. "It has to. I can't stand in the way of your happiness."

"What makes you think that being without you would make me happy? I don't see why this couldn't work. You're here until the end of summer. I can commute back here on weekends. Sure, I know we won't see as much of one another as we have but we can handle that, can't we?"

"And your wife? What will she have to say about that?"

"I have paid very handsomely to ensure that my *ex*-wife has nothing to say about my life at all." He crossed the short distance between them and cupped her face in his hands, tilting her head so she looked directly at him. "It was just a stupid rumor, Catherine. Don't you think that I would have treated you better than that? At least have had the courtesy to tell you if I wasn't divorced? Surely you must have understood that about me, if nothing else."

"I didn't know what to think. I couldn't help but notice she's always calling you. Besides, you know what it's like in the world I live in. People come and go. Love affairs are exactly that—affairs, with nothing more to them but a need to be together for however long before moving on to the next tournament or the next lover."

"I'm not like that. I love you. I couldn't walk away from you now, not for anything or anyone else." They were just words, she told herself, even as hope began to swell in her heart. She shook her head—she didn't dare to hope.

"I came here to have a vacation and maybe, yeah, sow some wild oats while I was here. I never expected to find you, to find love. I fought how I feel about you because I've just finalized an ugly and bitter divorce, which ended an equally ugly and bitter marriage. The last thing I was looking for was the person I want to spend the rest of my life with."

"It's a rebound thing, Richard. Be serious for a minute. What we have, it can't be real."

"Why not? It feels damn real to me. More real than anything I've ever felt or hoped for. I admit I rushed into my first marriage and regretted it deeply—still do, in fact. It wasn't fair to either of us, and it took well over a year to extricate myself from it. But this—" he pressed a kiss against her lips "—is so much more."

"How can you be sure?" Catherine asked, her voice quavering. "You admit yourself that you rushed into things the first time around. We've barely known each other four weeks! I spent the first week you were here trying to avoid you, for goodness' sake. People just don't fall in love that fast. Not forever."

"I did—once, with you. We haven't had much time together, but we have the rest of our lives to find out how well we fit."

"But don't you see? We're so different. Once you leave this, *my* world, we have nothing left in common but our physical attraction to one another. And that's not enough. It's never enough. I want more than that if I ever settle with someone. I *need* more than that. I lost everything once—my father, my home, my mother when she went away. I'm not prepared to take that risk again."

"Catherine, do you really think we're so very different? You want a home, a happier future—maybe even a family. What makes you think I don't want those things, too? I never looked past the moment with Daniella, but with you I want to look forward, and I see you there at my side."

Catherine shook her head again, trying to deny his words, but she couldn't deny how much she wanted them to be true. How much she wanted *him*.

"Listen to me, please," he implored her. "Let us at least give it a try. I know you need security. Let me prove to you that I can be the man to give it to you. That I will always be there for you. We can take this easy, keep seeing each other on weekends and whenever I can get away. Hell, I'll do whatever it takes to keep you, Catherine, even if it means signing over my share of Clearwater to Seb."

"No! Don't even think about that. You love your work. You love what the two of you have built together."

"Sure I do, but don't you see? I love you more. I worked hard at establishing Clearwater to spite my father, to prove him wrong. But it turns out I proved him right. He never doubted me—he just thought it was too soon. And maybe it's too soon for us, but I cannot walk away and think for one moment that we could never be together again. I want you in my life, Catherine. Forever."

She was shocked to see tears in his eyes.

"We'll take this as fast or as slow as you want to, but please, don't cut me out of your life. Even if it takes you the next year to be sure that you love me enough to marry me and spend the rest of your life with me. Even if it takes the next ten years."

She smiled a watery smile. "I think ten years might be a bit excessive. But Richard, I couldn't live in the city. I need my horses. I need to fulfill my dreams and my goals in life, too. You've done so much already in such a short time. Surely you can understand why this is important to me, too."

"I wouldn't expect you to live in the city. I can commute. There's a heliport right near my office. I want more than anything to see you attain your dreams. You wouldn't be you without them. But you can have your own stables and be my wife at the same time."

"My stables?" She gave a wry grin. "Like that's going to happen anytime soon. Maybe ten years isn't so much of a stretch after all. Scandal still hangs over my family name, Richard. You don't want that scandal attached to your name, as well."

"Scandal? Catherine, every part of my marriage was paraded through the media. I think I can handle it."

"But this is different. It's more than 'he said, she said.' It's the kind of thing that people don't forget."

"Which is why we're going to deal with it. We're going to clear your father's name once and for all—for *you*."

Catherine looked at him in shock. "But how?"

"I've already put an investigator on it. It's unlikely the people involved have changed all that much. Once we have proof, I'm sure with sufficient persuasion they can be induced to make a statement regarding your father's lack of involvement."

"You'd do that for me?" She was incredulous. No one had ever stood up for her like this. No one had looked after her in so very long.

"You gave me back my father. It's only fair I give you back yours."

All shreds of weariness fell away from her. He loved her. He truly loved her. And, more importantly, he was free to do so. Catherine threw her arms around him, burying her face in his neck.

"I love you so much. It was killing me to have to let you go. I didn't want to believe you were still married or that you could be married and still make love with me."

"So you're prepared to give us a try? To take things slow?"

She pulled back and looked him square in the eyes.

"No. I don't want to take things slow. I've waited this long for someone special in my life. I don't want to waste another minute. Is that okay?"

Richard's lips curved into a beautiful smile that was all the answer she needed.

Forever.

* * * * *

Don't miss the next anthology in
"A Summer for Scandal"
IN TOO DEEP
Featuring stories from New York Times *and* USA
Today *bestselling author Brenda Jackson*
and Olivia Gates
Available July 13, 2010
From Silhouette Desire

COMING NEXT MONTH

Available July 13, 2010

#2023 THE MILLIONAIRE MEETS HIS MATCH
Kate Carlisle
Man of the Month

#2024 CLAIMING HER BILLION-DOLLAR BIRTHRIGHT
Maureen Child
Dynasties: The Jarrods

#2025 IN TOO DEEP
"Husband Material"—Brenda Jackson
"The Sheikh's Bargained Bride"—Olivia Gates
A Summer for Scandal

#2026 VIRGIN PRINCESS, TYCOON'S TEMPTATION
Michelle Celmer
Royal Seductions

#2027 SEDUCTION ON THE CEO'S TERMS
Charlene Sands
Napa Valley Vows

#2028 THE SECRETARY'S BOSSMAN BARGAIN
Red Garnier

REQUEST YOUR FREE BOOKS!

2 FREE NOVELS PLUS 2 FREE GIFTS!

Passionate, Powerful, Provocative!

YES! Please send me 2 FREE Silhouette Desire® novels and my 2 FREE gifts (gifts are worth about $10). After receiving them, if I don't wish to receive any more books, I can return the shipping statement marked "cancel." If I don't cancel, I will receive 6 brand-new novels every month and be billed just $4.05 per book in the U.S. or $4.74 per book in Canada. That's a saving of at least 15% off the cover price! It's quite a bargain! Shipping and handling is just 50¢ per book.* I understand that accepting the 2 free books and gifts places me under no obligation to buy anything. I can always return a shipment and cancel at any time. Even if I never buy another book, the two free books and gifts are mine to keep forever.

225/326 SDN E5QG

Name	(PLEASE PRINT)	
Address		Apt. #
City	State/Prov.	Zip/Postal Code

Signature (if under 18, a parent or guardian must sign)

Mail to the **Silhouette Reader Service:**
IN U.S.A.: P.O. Box 1867, Buffalo, NY 14240-1867
IN CANADA: P.O. Box 609, Fort Erie, Ontario L2A 5X3

Not valid for current subscribers to Silhouette Desire books.

Want to try two free books from another line?
Call 1-800-873-8635 or visit www.morefreebooks.com.

* Terms and prices subject to change without notice. Prices do not include applicable taxes. N.Y. residents add applicable sales tax. Canadian residents will be charged applicable provincial taxes and GST. Offer not valid in Quebec. This offer is limited to one order per household. All orders subject to approval. Credit or debit balances in a customer's account(s) may be offset by any other outstanding balance owed by or to the customer. Please allow 4 to 6 weeks for delivery. Offer available while quantities last.

Your Privacy: Silhouette Books is committed to protecting your privacy. Our Privacy Policy is available online at www.eHarlequin.com or upon request from the Reader Service. From time to time we make our lists of customers available to reputable third parties who have a product or service of interest to you. If you would prefer we not share your name and address, please check here. ☐

Help us get it right—We strive for accurate, respectful and relevant communications. To clarify or modify your communication preferences, visit us at www.ReaderService.com/consumerchoice.

SDES10R

HARLEQUIN®

A Romance

FOR EVERY MOOD™

Spotlight on

— Heart & Home —

Heartwarming romances
where love can happen
right when you least expect it.

See the next page to enjoy a sneak peek
from Silhouette Special Edition®,
a Heart and Home series.

*Introducing McFARLANE'S PERFECT BRIDE
by USA TODAY bestselling author Christine Rimmer,
from Silhouette Special Edition®.*

Entranced. Captivated. Enchanted.

Connor sat across the table from Tori Jones and
couldn't help thinking that those words exactly described
what effect the small-town schoolteacher had on him.
He might as well stop trying to tell himself he wasn't
interested. He was powerfully drawn to her.

Clearly, he should have dated more when he was
younger.

There had been a couple of other women since Jennifer
had walked out on him. But he had never been entranced.
Or captivated. Or enchanted.

Until now.

He wanted her—*her,* Tori Jones, in particular. Not just
someone suitably attractive and well-bred, as Jennifer had
been. Not just someone sophisticated, sexually exciting
and discreet, which pretty much described the two women
he'd dated after his marriage crashed and burned.

It came to him that he...he *liked* this woman. And that
was new to him. He liked her quick wit, her wisdom and
her big heart. He liked the passion in her voice when she
talked about things she believed in.

He liked *her.* And suddenly it mattered all out of
proportion that she might like him, too.

Was he losing it? He couldn't help but wonder. Was
he cracking under the strain—of the soured economy, the
McFarlane House setbacks, his divorce, the scary changes
in his son? Of the changes he'd decided he needed to make
in his life and himself?

Strangely, right then, on his first date with Tori Jones, he didn't care if he just might be going over the edge. He was having a great time—having *fun,* of all things—and he didn't want it to end.

Is Connor finally able to admit his feelings to Tori, and are they reciprocated?
Find out in McFARLANE'S PERFECT BRIDE
by USA TODAY *bestselling author Christine Rimmer.*
Available July 2010,
only from Silhouette Special Edition®.